THE STARTING ELEVEN

DAVID SKUY

JAMES LORIMER & COMPANY LTD., PUBLISHERS

TORONTO

James Lorimer & Company Ltd., Publishers acknowledges the support of the Ontario Arts Council. We acknowledge the support of the Canada Council for the Arts which last year invested $24.3 million in writing and publishing throughout Canada. We acknowledge the Government of Ontario through the Ontario Media Development Corporation's Ontario Book Initiative.

Cover design: Tyler Cleroux
Cover image: Shutterstock

Library and Archives Canada Cataloguing in Publication

Skuy, David, 1963-, author
    The starting eleven / David Skuy.

Issued in print and electronic formats.
ISBN 978-1-4594-1132-6 (paperback).--ISBN 978-1-4594-1133-3 (epub)
        I. Title.

PS8637.K72S73 2016   jC813'.6   C2016-902635-3
                                                      C2016-902636-1

James Lorimer &
Company Ltd., Publishers
117 Peter Street, Suite
304
Toronto, ON, Canada
M5V 0M3
www.lorimer.ca

Canadian edition
(978-1-4594-1132-6)
distributed by:
Formac Lorimer Books
5502 Atlantic Street
Halifax, NS, Canada
B3H 1G4

American edition
(978-1-4594-1135-7)
distributed by:
Lerner Publishing Group
1251 Washington Ave N
Minneapolis, MN, USA
55401

Canadian edition printed and bound in Canada.
United States edition printed and bound in Canada.
Manufactured by Friesens Corporation in Altona, Manitoba, Canada in July 2016.
Job #225184

*As with soccer, a book series requires a great team to make
something happen. I was fortunate to have that team.
Thanks to all of you for joining me on Cody's journey.*

Thud!

"Get to the ball first, Cody," Coach Trevor yelled. "Play like it's a game, not a practice. This is Major, not house league."

Cody Dorsett took off down the right wing. His lungs bursting and his legs aching, he desperately wanted to rest. It was just a team practice after all. Luca, the outside left defender, was barrelling over to head him off. Cody stretched out his left foot and flicked the ball to the right.

Luca's chest hit him full-on and both boys fell to the ground.

"The team name is the Lions, not the Pussycats. Get up," Trevor said.

Cody struggled to his knees and brought the ball under control with his left foot. Luca sprung up and lunged for the ball. Cody pushed with his right foot and hand to lift himself up, just enough to shield the ball. Luca knocked him toward the sidelines, but Cody was able to keep his feet and drag the ball with him. His back to Luca, Cody head faked toward the goal line. Then he spun to his right, curling to the middle of the field. He had opened up some space.

"Move the ball," Trevor said.

"Cody!" Kenneth yelled. The Lions centre midfielder cut into the box.

Jordan, a forward like Cody, waved his hand. He'd set up for a cross near the far post.

"I'm here," another player called.

That was Paulo, the Lions third forward. He was about five yards back.

Should Cody shoot? Cross to Jordan? Take a chance inside to Kenneth? Or the simple pass to Paulo? For the briefest of moments everything seemed to slow down. He could see it now — so obvious. All but one of the passes were too high risk.

Cody gave it to Paulo.

"Good play," Trevor said, with a quick nod. "Don't give the ball away with dumb passes."

That feels better, Cody thought. Trevor didn't offer many compliments.

"You still suck, Dorsett," Luca muttered as he brushed past him.

Cody laughed. They were good friends but fierce competitors. They were playing half-field, with the three forwards and two midfielders attacking against the four

Lions defenders and a midfielder, with David, their goalie, in net. Everyone was going full-out.

"Ring it around," Cody shouted.

Paulo slipped the ball to Brandon, who punched it inside to Kenneth. Kenneth drifted left and fed Jordan at the far side. Kenneth cut back and took a pass from Jordan five feet from the box. When William and Luca collapsed on him, Kenneth had to give it up to Cody in the middle of the field.

"It's five-on-five," Trevor called out. "Attacking side, you need to create overlaps and support in groups of three. You're too spread out and trying to attack as individuals."

"Come on, forwards, stop being such losers," Luca mocked.

They'd been at it for half the practice and the forwards hadn't scored yet. The defenders weren't giving them anything to shoot at. When they did have a chance, their goalkeeper David was there with his usual acrobatics to keep the ball out.

"To you, Paulo," Cody said. He sent the ball to his right.

Paulo handled it nimbly, inching the ball with the outside of his right boot. He looked inside and raised his eyebrows ever so slightly.

Cody saw it too — a gap between Luca and William. Cody knew that Paulo could see it too. Finally, a chance! Cody took a few short steps toward the goal. Then, without warning, he broke into a full sprint into the gap. Paulo arced the ball around Luca's left leg. Cody took a quick glance at Jordan, who had beaten his man on the left. David had come out to take away the angle.

7

Cross or shoot?

Again, the game slowed down for Cody. He knew the right play. He glanced again at Jordan. He didn't want to look like a ball hog. He took another step and then drove his right leg into the ball. David left his feet and threw his right arm out. The ball grazed his fingers and skidded outside the post.

Cody jumped up and slapped his hands together in frustration. Almost! He took another kick with his right leg.

"Not even close," Luca chuckled. "Coach, can we get some real forwards? These guys are pathetic."

"How dare you call me a pathetic forward?" Kenneth glared. "I'm a useless midfielder — and so is Brandon."

Luca slapped his thighs with his hands. "I can never keep that straight. The midfielders on this team are useless. It's the forwards who are pathetic."

"That was a nice set-up," Trevor said, coming over to Cody. "Not sure why you hesitated on that shot. David was caught in no man's land trying to guard against the cross to Jordan. A quicker shot might've scored. Your passing is beautiful, love it. But you're a striker. Your job is to score. A striker has to be like a hunter, like a predator stalking its prey."

"Sorry, Coach," Cody said. "I thought about chipping across to Jordan, then changed my mind. Stupid, because I knew the right play was to shoot. Awesome pass, Paulo. I wasted it."

"Keep the game simple, Cody. Always pass to me," Kenneth said.

"Soccer used to be simple." Cody laughed. "Now it's

about triangularity, ball possession, angles, and overlaps. Not sure I'll ever figure it out."

"Coach, I think you should ask Cody to leave. Bad enough he's a pathetic striker. But I will not accept him not passing to me all the time," Kenneth said. "And now would be a good time to compliment me on my awesomeness."

Trevor's eyes grew brighter, and the corners of his mouth curled up. "I'll take a rain check on that, but thanks for offering. As for Cody leaving, there is that troublesome fact that we only have eleven players. We'd have to default the rest of our games. And I kind of wanted to see if we would make the playoffs — and win the championship."

"I have a better idea. We could ask Timothy and John to come back and play for us," David said.

His joking suggestion made Luca groan. "Why not ask all the guys who ruined our lives and then quit on us? I really miss being abused by Antonio and Tyler and Michael too."

"Let's get Ian to be our manager again. He can bench us and we can keep losing all our games," Kenneth said. "Please, Coach, can we do it? I liked losing."

"Maybe another time." Trevor grinned. "For now, Timothy and his friends can keep playing on the Storm, and Ian can keep managing them. How about we get back to the drill? It's crunch time, lads. Playoffs are around the corner. Four games left, and we're battling it out with the Clippers, AFC, and South. Our bad start to the season is hurting us. We can't really afford to lose a game the rest of the way," Trevor said.

"We wouldn't have lost those seven games in a row if Timothy and those jerks had just quit earlier," Kenneth said.

"Let's not worry about the Storm," Trevor said. He paused. "But couldn't you have made them leave before the season started?"

The boys laughed.

"First stop are the Flames," Luca said. "Let's douse them with a little Lion-ade, and then bring it home."

"Well punned, my empty-headed defender," Kenneth said. "Lions on three! One – two – three!"

The boys answered as one.

"Roar!"

Trevor's gaze drifted to the sidelines and a big smile crossed his face. "Hold up a minute. I invited someone out to practise with us, and it looks like he's arrived." Trevor jogged away.

William flicked his chin at the sidelines. "What's this about inviting a player out? Isn't it too late in the season to add guys?"

"It would be sweet to have a sub," Kenneth said. "Then we could get Luca's useless and pathetic butt off the field."

Luca looked around at his teammates. "Who told him I was useless and pathetic? That was a secret." He pretended to wipe away a tear.

On the sidelines, Trevor shook hands with a tall man, a little heavy, with a bit of a stomach and really thick black eyebrows. He wore a long, pale blue shirt with buttons down the front and no collar. Next to him stood a small, thin woman with long black hair in a single braid down her back. Two other men stood to the side. They were more athletic-looking, both wearing track pants and sweatshirts. One of them caught Cody's attention because he wore a yellow hoodie with the Lions crest on the front.

A kid stepped forward and shook Trevor's hand. He wore a blue track suit, with three black stripes down the side — and he wore soccer cleats. He and Trevor ran back to the field.

"Listen up," Trevor said, as he and the kid approached. "Let me introduce Mustafa."

"It's Stafa. Only my mom — and grandma — call me that," the boy said.

Up close he looked a little like the man with the thick eyebrows. But his face was more delicate and thin, like the woman's. Cody figured he was their son.

"We'll stick with Stafa, then." Trevor laughed. "Stafa plays for the Lions in the Premier league, in the twelve-year-old division. You may recognize the fellow on the sidelines, with the yellow hoodie. That's Benji, Stafa's coach, and next to him is Ed, his assistant coach. Benji thought it might be a good experience for Stafa to play with us. I thought we'd all love to have a sub, so I invited him out for the practice."

"Sorry I'm late," Stafa said. "Our game didn't start on time."

"You're sure you aren't tired?" Trevor said.

Stafa shrugged. "The other team sucked. It was 5 – 0 by half-time. I stopped running after ten minutes. I'm good."

Premier was a league up from Major, but Cody was surprised by Stafa's confidence. Stafa was a year younger than Cody, but he didn't act like it.

"We're allowed to add players this late in the season?" Kenneth said.

"We're allowed to add up to two players for the last five games," Trevor explained. "But only if they're already playing for a Lions team. And they have to be either moving up a division or, as in this case, be younger than the team they're moving to."

"What position do you play?" Paulo asked.

Cody felt a tug in his stomach. The question hung in the air.

"Striker," Stafa said simply. "I've always been a striker."

Striker? That was Cody's position. Cody looked down at the ground and kicked at a piece of dirt. Was Trevor trying to tell him something?

"Let's keep going with the drill," Trevor said. "Defenders are doing a great job keeping their legs active and cutting off passing lanes. Forwards, you have to do a better job supporting each other. Passes are too flat. You need to create angles and then run onto the ball, at pace, to get the defenders nervous about holding the line. So let's set up." He pressed his lips together and closed his eyes momentarily. "Hey, Cody, how about giving Stafa a chance to join in with the forwards. You've been working hard this practice. Have a seat and I'll sub you in later."

"Okay," Cody managed.

Message received.

"Good. Just hang tight," Trevor said. He blew his whistle

and threw a ball toward the far sidelines. "Retrieve and attack!" he yelled.

Paulo ran to get the ball. The defenders scrambled to get into position.

"Just do your best," Trevor said to Stafa. "No pressure."

"No worries, Coach. I'm psyched," Stafa said. He sprinted off to the far right.

Paulo passed to Stafa right off. Stafa spun with the ball on the outside of his left foot and then punched it to Jordan near the sidelines.

"I'm going to get some water," Cody said to Trevor.

Trevor didn't hear, preoccupied with the drill. Cody walked slowly to the sidelines.

"Nice support, Stafa," Trevor said, his hands cupped around his mouth.

Stafa followed his pass up. Jordan gave it back to him. Benji, Ed, and Stafa's parents were by the corner flag. Most of the other parents had left to run errands, or to do whatever adults did when their kids were practising. Even Cody's mom was somewhere else, which was sort of a miracle. Usually she stayed, and embarrassed him by watching like a hawk and asking if he was okay if someone so much as bumped into him.

Cody got why she was like that. Any mom would be protective if they had a kid get sick — let alone with cancer. This was probably the first time his mom had brought him to a practice and didn't watch — a good sign, hopefully. He touched the back of his right leg where the tumour had been. It didn't feel any different from his left.

Cody walked over to where everyone had piled their

bags. He shivered. The wind made him cold when he wasn't running around. He reached over and grabbed his sweatshirt and a water bottle from his bag.

Stafa was a striker on the Lions twelve-year-olds Premier team, so obviously he was a pretty good player. Cody's Lions had three forwards already — Cody, Jordan, and Paulo. Paulo was an amazing player, so obviously he wasn't going to sit. Cody had scored the most goals on the team, though. Jordan took all the corners and free kicks. Who would Trevor sit? Obviously him today. Why add new guys, anyway? Sure, it was hard to play with only eleven. They were one injury away from having to default. But they'd done okay. The Lions were tied for sixth, and the top six teams made the playoffs.

Cody put his water bottle back in his bag. He watched Stafa. The kid could run, had to give him that. And his ball skills were pretty good. Cody wrapped his arms around his knees and dropped his chin. Funny how he'd been tired of the drill, and now he was dying to get back out there.

A man's voice caught Cody's attention.

"I knew it. I knew it. That Trevor is a total sneak."

Cody knew that voice. And it always meant trouble.

Cody snuck a look up over the pile of bags. It was Ian, Timothy's father, who used to manage the Lions. John's father, Mitch, was with him. Timothy and John were the Lions forwards, until they quit. Cody pressed up against the bags and ducked his head. He prayed they wouldn't see him.

"Smartest thing I ever did was transfer Timmer from those Lions jokers," Ian said.

"John's not . . . the happiest with the Storm."

"Mitch, I'm not dealing with that again. John has to work harder if he wants to earn playing time. Tough lesson. But life's tough," Ian snapped.

Cody used to think Timothy and John were best friends. He'd run into them a few times since they'd left the Lions, at games and around town. Cody had noticed that Timothy bullied John a lot; and like their sons, Ian sorta bullied Mitch too.

Cody had begun to feel a bit sorry for John. But he sure didn't feel sorry for Timothy. Timothy was always teasing Cody with choice nicknames — Humpty Dumpty, Cue Ball, Egg-Head. It was a few months since Cody's hair had fallen out after his cancer treatments, but Timothy and his friends never lost a chance to remind him of the fact that he looked different.

"I'm going to the league commissioner on this one," Ian said. "José will do what he's told. That's Mustafa Unsal playing. No way he's allowed to join a team in Major. He's in Premier."

"I think it's because the boy is a year younger and —"

"Don't be dumb," Ian said. "Premier is Premier. It's not allowed."

"You're right. For sure. Still, if José doesn't agree, the Lions will be tough to beat. They're tough already — and that Unsal kid is unstoppable. Once I saw him score six goals in one game," Mitch said.

"Timothy once scored ten goals in a game, when he was six years old, so I don't care what Unsal did. No one can stop Timothy. Kid's on fire this year, and he'll be playing Premier next year, too. Put money on it," Ian said.

Mitch cleared his throat. "I thought you wanted to keep the Storm together and —"

"Just shut up about it, would ya? Keep it to yourself for once. Can you do that? Timmer's too good for Major. Kid with that kind of talent belongs in Premier. Not my fault the other kids can't keep up."

Cody heard footsteps approaching and ducked further down.

"Ian . . . Mitch . . . How are you?"

Cody peered around the bags. It was Benji and Ed, along with Stafa's parents.

Ian gave Benji an angry look. "Are you guys serious about Unsal playing for Trevor?"

Benji laughed, but he looked uncomfortable. "This is Gary and Rita, Stafa's parents," Benji said.

Gary didn't seem all that interested. After shaking Ian's and Mitch's hands, he began to watch the drill intently.

"Nothing personal against Stafa, but it's too late in the year to transfer," Ian said.

"Same organization," Benji said.

"He's Premier," Ian said.

"He's a year younger," Benji said.

"That's what I thought," Mitch said.

"Yeah . . . Thanks, Mr. Two-Cents," Ian hissed at Mitch. He turned back to Benji. "Okay. Okay," Ian said, his tone suddenly friendly. "Let's change the subject. I've heard some rumours, talk around town. You're maybe submitting a Premier team next season, Timothy's age?"

"Maybe," Benji said. "Like you said, it's just talk at this stage."

"Well . . . Timothy's looking around. He's getting some offers and stuff. I know teams can't actually make formal offers yet, but you know how things happen. Anyway, maybe we can work out a deal. I let this go, and you take a look at Timothy for next season," Ian said.

"I don't think we've done anything wrong. But I'm

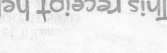

EcoChit ∴ veritree

BPA/BPS Free   Recyclable   Sustainably Sourced

This receipt helps plant a forest.
(scan to learn more)

happy to take a look at your kid, obviously," Benji said.

"I have some resources, sponsorships and stuff," Ian said. "We'll talk. Here's my card. This might actually work out okay. For sure. I'm liking this. We'll talk. Definitely."

Benji took Ian's card.

"I gotta get ready for our practice," Ian said. "We're on the field next. Mitch, do you have the drills written out?"

"Shoot. I forgot my tablet in the car," Mitch said.

"Smart, Sherlock. It's doing a lot of good there," Ian said.

"Good to see you," Benji said softly. "Excuse us. We should watch the last few minutes."

"Nice to meet you," Rita said.

She joined Gary and the two coaches.

"I'll go get the drills," Mitch said. He began to walk to the parking lot.

Cody's heart began racing a second time. Timothy and John were walking toward Ian.

"Where're you going, Dad?" John said, as Mitch passed them.

"I forgot something . . . in the car," Mitch said.

"Like your brain?" Timothy said loudly.

Ian laughed.

"You guys chill for a second," Ian said to Timothy and John. "I have to ask Benji something. Hey, Benji, Ed. Hold up. I have an idea about that thing we were talking about."

Ian shuffled off. Cody snuck another look. His stomach lurched. Three more Storm players were coming — Antonio, Tyler, and Michael. This was great. The five guys who bullied him non-stop when they were on the Lions were going to see him hiding like a scared little boy.

"Look who's practising," Timothy said to his teammates.

"It's the Geek Squad," Tyler said.

Cody sometimes wondered if he was the unluckiest kid in the world.

Timothy nodded at the bags. "I bet that's the Lions' stuff. I got an idea." he said.

"What?" John said.

"What? What?" Timothy mocked. "You guys cover me. I gotta pee."

"You can't practise with a full bladder." Tyler laughed.

"That's dangerous." Michael giggled.

"That's a bit . . . gross," John said.

"Shut up, wuss, and just stand here and give me cover. I've got this," Timothy said.

Cody gritted his teeth and clenched his fists. It was just like Timothy to pee all over their bags, like a dog. But Cody wasn't going to be Timothy's personal fire hydrant. He ran a hand over his head. His hair had come back a bit. It wasn't close to grown in, though. He tried to think of an insult, like what Kenneth or Luca or Paulo would say in this situation. He stood up.

"Washrooms are over there," Cody said, pointing to a building by the road.

"Did he pop out of the ground?" Antonio said.

"He looks like a weasel, so maybe," Tyler said.

"It's the one and only Humpty Dumpty," Timothy said.

"What a surprise. Didn't expect that," Cody said to Timothy.

He tried to keep his voice low and calm.

Antonio elbowed Timothy. "They bench you, Egg-Head? I guess Trevor finally figured out how much you suck."

"Always thought Eggy would make a better water boy than striker," Timothy said. "You wanna fetch me some water? I'm thirsty."

"I wouldn't have that water," Cody said to Timothy. "I know you have trouble with toilet training. And you have a hard time keeping your diaper on."

John smirked and covered his face with his hand.

Timothy shot him an angry look. John turned red. Cody let himself smile. That wasn't bad. He wished his teammates could've heard it.

"Timmer, come over here," Ian called out. "I want you to meet someone."

"Sure, Mr. Pain in the Butt," Timothy said under his breath. He turned and waved back. "Okay. Hold on," he said loudly to his dad.

"I shouldn't waste my pee on you, Baldy," Timothy said to Cody. "John, go give him a hug. I think he's gonna start crying." He walked off.

"Keep in touch," Antonio said.

He and the rest of them followed Timothy, except for John. Cody and John's eyes locked for a moment. John never looked happy when Cody saw him.

"You shouldn't let them bug you," Cody said. "They're all talk."

But Cody knew how much that talk could hurt. He had almost quit playing with the Lions, before Trevor took over the team, because of their bullying.

John kicked at the ground. "Not much I can do about it," he said.

21

Cody wanted to say something to make him feel better. "The Storm is going good. You'll probably finish in second place."

Not the most inspiring thing to say.

"We'll never beat United," John said. "I think you guys could do it, though."

John's compliment caught Cody off guard. "We have to make the playoffs first," Cody said. "But United's gonna be tough, for sure."

"You can beat them," John said.

"Maybe. So see you in the playoffs, I guess," Cody said.

John managed a weak smile. "I never play. I'm the one who's a sub now."

Funny how they'd switched places. John used to start for the Lions while Cody sat on the bench. John looked over to the parking lot. Mitch was struggling to carry two big string bags filled with soccer balls, his iPad stuffed under his arm. John's shoulders slumped.

"Have a good practice. I'll see you around," Cody said.

"Thanks. See ya," John said, and he jogged off to help his dad.

Cody watched him go, a little saddened by it. Timothy had this way of getting to you and making you feel bad about yourself. Cody felt a little proud. He'd stood up for himself. Timothy would never make him feel bad about himself again. John couldn't get away from Timothy, though. Maybe Cody wasn't the unluckiest kid in the world?

Cody pushed his kit bag under his bed. The drive home from practice had been quiet. He was preoccupied with the idea that the Lions would have a new player. Eventually, his mom had given up trying to talk to him and had turned on the radio.

Stafa could play, no question. Cody sighed and pushed it from his mind. Kenneth had just messaged him that some of the guys were heading to Lake Tawson this afternoon, which was cool. It was weird he hadn't been back to the lake in a few weeks. This summer he'd practically lived at the lake for three weeks to protest the building of a factory there. Still hard to believe they'd helped stop it by playing a marathon soccer game — and even harder to believe the game had been his idea. The Marathon Game became an Internet sensation, practically going viral, and it attracted a ton of attention to the anti-factory protest. A warm glow passed through him.

Lake Tawson was important to him. When he was sick, he liked to go there, even when it was cold. He'd sit on the sand and watch the waves and feel the wind blow against his face. It gave him strength — the strength to fight the cancer. Saving the lake seemed like a signal that he'd put the cancer behind him.

Maybe it was all in his head. Made him feel better, though. He went downstairs to the kitchen. "I've made a sandwich for you," his mom said. "But eat up quickly. I have a meeting with a client in half an hour."

Things were hectic enough when only his mom worked from home. Now his dad had started a new business with some friends. He worked from home too. Sometimes Cody thought he lived in an office tower, with people coming and going all the time.

"No problem, Mom. I'm meeting up with some guys at Lake Tawson. Kenneth messaged me. I'll take this with me," Cody said.

"You can sit for a few minutes and eat properly," she said. "So who's going?"

Typical Mom question.

He wasn't sure why her questions bothered him. They just did. Not like the answers were a big secret.

"The usual," he offered.

She raised an eyebrow. "Kenneth, Luca, Paulo?"

"Yup."

"And the girls?"

"Not sure. Maybe?"

A surge of nervous energy shot through him. Mandy might be there. She would be if Kenneth invited Talia, her best friend. Those girls had helped organize the Marathon Game, and Kenneth was buds with Talia. Cody hadn't seen Mandy since the Marathon Game ended. They'd messaged each other a few times, and then she just stopped answering him. Cody thought Mandy and he had become buds too — or at least kinda like good friends. But now he wasn't so sure. Girls can be hard to figure out.

"Okay," his mom said, "but you can eat like a human being. Sit."

He sat at the table and began to eat quickly.

"Slow down and chew, or you'll make yourself sick," she said.

"I'm hungry."

"Did someone say hungry?" his dad said.

He sat next to Cody and rubbed his stomach.

Cody liked having his dad around during the day. All three of them spent a lot of time together now — hanging out and talking, like a family. They'd always been a family, of course, but when he got cancer his dad began to spend way more time at the office. After it was all over and Cody was better, his dad admitted he had worked so much because he couldn't deal with Cody's illness. Cody understood about being too afraid of what might happen. It still hurt, though — his dad not being there. This was nicer.

"Sean, would you like a sandwich?" his mom said.

"Thanks, Cheryl. You don't have to . . . But if you're already in the kitchen and you have a loaf of bread in front of you . . ."

She laughed and began slicing the bread. "Your son wants to go to Lake Tawson with some friends this afternoon."

"Be back by five," his dad said. "We have dinner at Auntie Beth's tonight."

"Please tell me Adam and Sarah are still at summer camp," Cody pleaded. His cousins drove him crazy with the games they forced him to play — for hours.

"Good news," his mom said. "They both got home yesterday."

"When will those kids grow up already? It's like they're permanently little," Cody said.

She handed his dad the sandwich. "Cody forgot to mention there will be girls at the lake."

His dad sat up straight. "Hold on a minute. Girls?" His dad got a mischievous look on his face. "Should I come along to make sure nothing happens?"

"It's just Mandy and Talia — they're not like . . ." His voice trailed off. "We might play some soccer. It's good to practise against them—they play Premier."

"Gotcha." His dad winked.

Cody rolled his eyes. Parents were so lame about girls, like it was a big deal. Besides, he didn't think of Talia and Mandy like that.

"How is Mandy?" Cheryl said. "You haven't mentioned her lately."

"She's fine," Cody mumbled, taking a bite of his sandwich.

"And Talia?"

"She's good too."

He pushed his plate away. His mom would ask a million more questions about why he hadn't spoken to Mandy in a while. No big thing. Without the Marathon Game, maybe Mandy figured they didn't have much to talk about.

"Thanks, Mom. That was good. I was hungrier than I thought."

He took his dish and cup to the sink and rinsed them off. He wished his mom hadn't mentioned Mandy. Hearing her name upset him — and that bugged him.

"I guess I'll just grab my bike and make my way to the lake," Cody said.

The doorbell rang, followed by some pounding on the door.

"Cheryl, are your clients trying to break our door down?" Sean said.

"My clients tend to be civilized persons." She looked at Cody. "You wanna check it out?"

Cody poked his head out of the kitchen and looked down the hall. "I think it's the guys," he said. He hadn't expected them to come by.

"Be back at five o'clock," Sean said.

"If I had a phone, you could call me," Cody said.

"Wear your watch," Cheryl said.

He was probably the last kid in the world his age without a phone. Cody opened the door.

"YOLO," Kenneth said.

"No one says that anymore," Luca said.

"That's what makes it extra, super, awesomely cool," Kenneth said.

"Let's go, Cody. I need a normal guy to talk to," Paulo said.

"Don't use the word *normal* around Luca," Kenneth said. "He's sensitive about being so weird."

"I can't believe you think Cody's normal," Luca said to Paulo.

"I'm weirdly normal," Cody said.

"Great, so I'm the only actual normal guy here," Paulo said.

Cody headed to the garage for his bike.

"I got a ball, so we don't need yours," Paulo called out.

They went to the lake in a pack. Cody kept trying to think of a way to ask the question that had been torturing him since the practice. Finally, Luca did it for him.

"Where do you think Stafa's going to play?" Luca said.

"The obvious thing to do is take Austin off," Kenneth said.

Austin was a defender — and probably the weakest player on the team. Cody liked him, though. Austin never complained and he tried hard.

"I don't see Stafa playing back," Paulo said.

"Benji and Ed would have heart attacks," Kenneth said.

"Not really fair to Austin. He's been to every game and practice," Luca said.

"It's playoff time," Kenneth said. "Nothing personal, but don't we have to put out our best team? I mean . . . maybe Austin needs to drop down a level. I feel bad for him too."

Cody decided to put it out there. He'd been thinking about it long enough. "If Stafa's the new striker . . . and we need Jordan for corners and free kicks . . ."

They surprised him by laughing.

"Not likely, Mailman," Kenneth said.

Cody smiled at Kenneth's nickname for him. Kenneth

said it was because Cody always delivered a goal when they needed one.

"Where's he going to play, then?" Cody said.

"Austin will sit. Ryan or Brandon will move back, and Stafa will sub in at midfield," Luca said. "Trust me. Trevor won't mess with you up front."

"Jordan will drop back, if anyone," Kenneth said.

"I guess," Cody said.

"Let's boogie, boys," Kenneth said, standing up and pedalling hard. "I told the girls we'd be there already. Talia practically begged me to drag you losers along."

The boys put it in high gear. Cody started to feel nervous again. Mandy would be there. Her face popped into his mind and he smiled. She wasn't like most of the other girls he knew. She kinda dressed like a boy and she was as serious about soccer as any kid on the Lions, including him. There was something about her, though. He could talk to her, and they had a connection he could never have with other kids. He'd had cancer, and Mandy's brother Gavin had died from cancer. Mandy understood how serious it was. It was impossible to explain that to a healthy kid. He'd thought about that a lot and couldn't help asking himself why he had lived and not Gavin.

"We're plugging up a weak spot in the lineup," Kenneth said to him. "I think Stafa's a good thing."

"We were doing okay . . . with the original eleven," Cody said. "Why change, is my question?"

They turned left and pressed on toward the hill that led to the lake. Cody didn't want Kenneth to think he was being selfish. He gathered his courage.

"I don't have a problem sitting or moving positions," Cody said. "But it breaks up the team a bit. And Stafa could mess things up."

"Or make things better?" Kenneth said.

"You boys realize I'm winning the race," Luca said over his shoulder.

Cody decided to drop it. He'd find out tomorrow. Besides, he wasn't about to lose a race, at least not without trying. He lowered his gear and powered on.

Winning wasn't the only thing, but it sure beat losing!

Cody trailed behind as the boys made their way across the beach toward the lake where Talia and Mandy were waiting.

"Which one of you is going to apologize first for being late?" Talia said.

"Probably Luca," Kenneth said. "I'm perfect, so it can't be my fault."

"I'm sorry Kenneth's perfect and made us all late," Luca said.

"How's it going, Mandy?" Cody said, walking up to where Mandy was standing.

"It's all fabulous," she said.

Mandy was looking out at the horizon. She wore a grey sack hat with her hair tucked under, baggy grey shorts and a soccer shirt, as usual, and two gold bracelets. Cody had never seen her wear jewellery before.

"Weird being here," Cody said to her. "I haven't been back since we finished with the Marathon Game."

Mandy puffed out her cheeks and shrugged.

"Kinda stupid that I haven't come," Cody continued. "We practically killed ourselves to stop them from building the factory, played soccer here for hours, and you with your Facebook page and tweets, not to mention all those people joining us. And . . ."

Mandy shrugged again. Cody could have kicked himself. She wasn't interested in his babbling.

The wind picked up. Cody breathed in the warm air and it made him cough. It was here, walking from the beach to the parking lot, that Mandy had told him that Gavin had died of leukemia and that her parents had split up after that. He wondered how he'd feel if that had happened to him. What if someone in his family got cancer instead of him? What if his parents got divorced?

"How are things . . .? I mean . . . What have you and Talia been . . . like . . . doing?" Cody's voice faded.

"I don't do anything," she said.

"Well . . . I haven't done much . . ." His mind whirled. Worst conversation ever. He needed to say something that wasn't totally boring. He looked to the forest. Mandy's mom, Candice, used to come before each Marathon Game to string up a big tarp for them to sit under during breaks. He remembered Mandy said they had the tarp because her family liked camping.

"Did you go camping this year, with your mom . . .?" he started.

She half laughed. "No camping with Mommy, not this summer."

"How come?"

"'Cause."

She walked past him and rejoined the others. Cody bit his lip and gave his head a shake.

"How're the Lions doing?" Talia was saying. "We've had three tournaments in a row and a bunch of games and practices on top of that."

Cody looked out over the water. A few birds were hovering offshore. Birds had it the best. They could just take off and leave if they didn't like where they were. Cody felt stuck. He'd never felt that way at the lake before.

"The Lions report is fairly good," Luca said. "We're back on track. We've won four in a row."

"Three teams are basically tied for the last two playoff spots, and another team is close too. It'll be tight," Kenneth said.

"We'll win," Luca said.

"So inspirational," Kenneth said.

"We won't win?" Luca said.

"Hmm, not so inspirational." Kenneth stuck his nose close to Luca and sniffed. "More like perspirational."

"We'd better make the playoffs," Paulo said. "My dad told me we're flying home to Brazil the day after the season ends."

Cody's mouth gaped open. How had he forgotten? Paulo was only in town for the summer while his dad taught at the hospital, and summer was nearly over. Paulo was the first kid Cody had met here after moving away from Ferguson to be closer to the hospital for his cancer treatments.

Paulo flashed a toothy grin. "It sucks, but I made my dad promise to bring us back soon. In Brazil, we have two terms, one in February and one that starts in August. July is a holiday. I've missed some of the second term, so my folks want us to get back before I miss too much."

"School? Forget about it. I've been going for years and I'm still incredibly stupid," Kenneth said.

"That's true. He is," Luca said. "Actually, I am too."

Talia tolled her eyes at Kenneth and Luca. "I never thought about you going home, Paulo, which obviously you have to."

"Don't worry about it," Kenneth said. "We're going to kidnap him. Did you buy the rope?" he said to Luca.

"Kidnapping is serious," Luca said. "Can't we just stick to bank robbery?"

"We have to do it for the Lions," Kenneth said.

"Fine." Luca pouted. "But no more kidnapping after this." He paused. "Who am I kidding? I love a good kidnapping. Great way to meet people."

A chill drifted down Cody's back. Mandy's face had gone completely white and he could see she was fighting back tears. She was totally bummed about Paulo leaving. So that was it. She had a crush on Paulo. Stupid of him to ignore the obvious. Paulo was the chillest guy around, and an amazing soccer player. Of course Mandy would have a crush on him. Probably that was why she was wearing the bracelets — to look nice.

Cody felt dumb for thinking she cared about him like

that, for thinking they had this serious connection because of Gavin.

Mandy wiped her eyes with her fingers. Cody looked out at the water again. The birds had flown away. The season was almost over. He wouldn't see the guys much anymore, maybe not until next soccer season. He'd be going to a new school, where he didn't know anyone. Paulo, the closest thing to a best friend he had, would be half a world away.

More alone time for Cody Dorsett coming up.

"So much happened this summer," Paulo said. "To be honest, I never wanted to come. We were all mad at my dad. He kept saying it would be fun and we could practise our English and meet new people. I didn't believe him. Meeting you guys made it all good. Hey, Cody, remember when you got my ball back from those jerks in the park?"

"What happened?" Talia said.

"Nothing big," Cody said. "We met, Paulo and I, at the park. We were playing soccer and . . . I got his ball from some guys."

"Worst storytelling ever," Paulo interrupted. "I'd been here for about three weeks and didn't know anyone. I was totally bored and wanted to go home, and I bugged my mom and dad about it every day. Finally, my dad told me to go play soccer. I grabbed his ball, an awesome leather one from Brazil, and went to the park. Two guys, big guys, were playing basketball."

Cody noticed Mandy was listening closely.

"I was kicking the ball around and the two guys stole it," Paulo said.

"Why?" Mandy said.

"They could see I wasn't from here. The usual bullying stuff . . . " Paulo shrugged. "Anyway, I knew I couldn't deal with them both. So I hid behind some trees and waited for my chance to get the ball. That's when I saw Mister Cody Dorsett glide over to the court, scoop my ball up, and stuff it under his sweatshirt. At first I thought he was stealing it, but he gave it back to me."

"Cody, in super stealth mode," Kenneth said.

"They didn't notice me," Cody mumbled.

"Then Cody invited me to try out for the Lions," Paulo said.

"So you're to blame," Luca said to Cody.

Mandy smiled — for the first time. Cody kicked a stone into the lake.

"Then one day we were all at the park after a tournament game," Paulo said. "The same two guys tried to steal our ball again."

Kenneth struck a bodybuilder pose.

"Yeah, it got messy," Luca said. "But we kept the ball and they ran away."

"That's life when you're a mega-warrior dude," Kenneth said. "Girls, feel free to gush over me."

"Golly, you're so big and strong. I feel faint," Talia said, breathlessly. She put the back of her hand to her forehead.

Mandy crossed her arms and gave Talia a stern look.

"We have a game tomorrow," Kenneth said. "Maybe you guys can come and watch our amazing bodies in motion."

"Tomorrow isn't good," Mandy said.

Talia looked pained.

A wave washed up. Cody pressed his toes in the wet sand and made a deep impression.

"We should go, Talia," Mandy said.

"Umm . . . Yeah . . . I guess," Talia said.

Kenneth pulled his ball from his backpack. "Can I tempt you with a little soccer, perhaps?"

"We have to go. Thanks," Mandy said. She headed to the sand dune.

Talia hesitated. "Yeah, sorry. Next time," she said.

She hurried after Mandy.

Kenneth flipped the ball back and forth in his hands. "Might be no point playing keep-away. I'll have the ball all the time, and you guys will get mad and have temper tantrums and cry like babies. But we have nothing else to do."

He tossed the ball in the air.

Cody gathered himself to jump. He felt unsettled, though. He felt he'd lost something — something important. Was this what it was like to lose a friend — or maybe more than a friend?

With Paulo to his right, Cody charged the Flames ball carrier. Trevor had been on them to pressure the ball in numbers and to take away passing lanes with proper foot position. Paulo threw his right foot out and the left midfielder cut inside to get away. Cody swept across his path and stripped the ball cleanly.

"Call a foul for once," Ian bellowed.

The Storm were playing later but Ian, Mitch, and few of the other Storm dads had shown up early to watch the Lions game. They'd been on the referee since the opening whistle.

"Just give it to the Lions, why don't you?" Antonio's dad said.

Cody passed inside to Kenneth close to the centre dot. Brandon, the Lions left midfielder, swung wide left and

Kenneth delivered a clean ball to send him down the sideline.

"This ref's a joke," Ian said, throwing his hands in the air.

Cody didn't stick around to listen. He forced his tired legs to carry on. Brandon got close to the box before a defender challenged. Brandon slowed, faked inside, and then flicked the ball outside with his left foot. The defender stayed with him, so Brandon gave the ball up to Kenneth, who had hustled over in support. He carried it inside and then passed to Cody, who was ten feet from the box.

Cody had two choices: get the ball into the box for a chance at goal or set up outside and try to create a triangle with Brandon and Kenneth. Paulo hovered on the outer edge of the box next to a defender. Cody knew what he had to do.

"Set it up, Lions!" Cody yelled to throw off the Flames defence. Cody saw their back line relax ever so slightly. At that precise moment, Paulo took off. Cody back-heeled a blind pass between the Flames middle defenders. The crowd roared. Cody turned in time to see Paulo with the ball. It had been a crazy, high-risk pass — and it had worked.

The goalie came out to cut down the angle. For a second, Cody thought Paulo had taken it in too close. Cody knew not to underestimate the Brazilian ball wizard, however. Paulo kicked down at the bottom of the ball. Grass flew into the goalie's shins — and the ball popped practically straight up. The goalie was so surprised his feet slipped out from under him as he tried to throw his arms up. He leapt back in desperation. His fingertips touched the ball, but not enough to stop it from falling under the cross bar and in.

Paulo circled in front, a fist in the air. Cody met him at the far post.

"I knew you were going for goal," Cody said. He put an arm around his neck.

"Don't tell the ref we can read minds," Paulo said.

"That's what you mean by setting it up?" Kenneth laughed. He threw his arms across Cody's and Paulo's shoulders.

"Go big or go home," Jordan said, joining the huddle.

They all slapped hands and jogged back to centre. That goal felt good to Cody. It wasn't just that it put them up by one before the half. It also showed Trevor that he had a few goal-scoring tricks up his sleeve.

Luca was holding his hand down low by his knees. Cody gave it a slap.

"Well done, lads," Luca said. "I was getting nervous. A tie ain't no use to us."

The referee put the ball down for the kickoff. Luca hooked a thumb over his shoulder.

"Maybe I should play my position," Luca said. "See ya, forwards."

Luca backpedalled next to William on the left side.

"Stay focused, Lions," Kenneth said.

"Strong on the ball," Trevor said from the sidelines.

Cody saw Paulo's father, Leandro, lean in to say something to Trevor. Leandro helped out as an assistant coach when he had time. Trevor looked over at Stafa and nodded.

Was Stafa coming on for the second half? Cody turned his attention back to the Flames forwards. Their number nine was ordering his midfielders around. He'd been acting the superstar all game, yelling at his teammates and throwing his hands up in the air if they didn't pass to him.

Cody readied himself. Number nine was too busy telling people what to do to notice him. He slowly crept to the right along the circle until he was almost touching the centre line.

Tweet!

The Flames forward gave the ball to number nine. Head down, he took a step back with the ball. Cody exploded forward. Number nine passed back to the right midfielder. The ball never made it. Cody intercepted and flew past the midfielders, the ball on his foot, the Lions supporters urging him on.

"Stand firm, back line," a centre defender said.

"We'll see," Cody muttered.

The back line moved forward to pressure. Cody chipped the ball over their heads — and kept going full tilt. The defenders were caught off guard, and by the time they turned around, Cody had gathered the ball and was in the clear. Out of the corner of his eye he saw the left outside back charging hard to cut him off. Cody veered left to gain some time and to check if Jordan or Paulo were open.

Cody took another step and fired.

"Stupid, Cody," he huffed

The defender had extended his foot in time to deflect the ball wide. Two – nothing would have been so sweet. Now the Lions had to be careful and protect their slender lead.

The referee's whistle sounded — half-time. Cody kicked at some dirt. He should've shot right away.

Paulo and Kenneth waited for him at centre.

"I thought the point of the game is to put the round ball into that net down there," Kenneth said.

"You could've saved a lot of energy and let them keep it." Paulo grinned.

"I wanted to see how much I could miss by," Cody said. "Now I know."

Kenneth shook Cody's hand. "Congrats. Knowledge is power," Kenneth said.

Cody laughed. But he was mad at himself.

"Bring it in, lads," Trevor said.

Cody joined his teammates in a semicircle in front of their coaches.

"A bit slow on the ball," Trevor began.

Kenneth elbowed Luca. "He's talking to you," Kenneth said.

Cody chuckled.

"Cody, a little more serious, please," Trevor snapped.

Cody wanted to dig a hole and climb into it. Trevor *had* to see him the moment he was laughing?

"We should have at least one more goal, probably two," Trevor continued. "We're down to the wire here, lads. We can't fool around and rely on a one-goal lead. We've dominated possession and we don't have a lot to show for it."

"We might be looking for the perfect shot," Leandro jumped in. "Stop with the fancy plays. Drive the ball at the net and look for rebounds. When we make that extra pass, we give them time to block the shot. Get more aggressive and shoot, shoot, shoot."

Cody squeezed his hands together. Those comments were meant for him — extra steps, fancy passes . . . and not being serious enough.

"Defenders, remember to keep an eye on their number nine. He's their late call-up. He's said to have a wicked shot," Trevor said.

"I've played against him tons of times," Stafa said. "He's a hog, and he hates having a man on him. Push him around a bit, and he'll lose his cool and make mistakes. Or better yet, foul you."

Trevor smiled ever so slightly. "Let's just mark him closely," he said.

"Let me have a run at him, Coach. I'll get him so riled up he'll take a red card," Stafa said.

Trevor ran a hand across his chin. "Actually, I think we'll make a change. Stafa, you go on and play forward with Jordan. Cody, you drop back to right midfield, and Ryan will slide back as a defender. Austin, can I have you sit off this half?"

"No problem, Coach," Austin said.

Cody half turned so Trevor wouldn't see his face. Midfield? He'd never played midfield in his life. One missed shot and that's it, no more striker?

The boys had thought he was being funny on the way to the lake. Cody wasn't laughing now.

Tweet!

The referee stood at centre for the second half. He let loose another blast of his whistle. "Line up, boys," the ref barked.

Usually, Cody was psyched to start the second half. Now he was all nerves. How had he lost his striker spot so quickly? He noticed the shoelace on his right boot was undone. He leaned down to tie it up. A shadow flitted across his face, and Trevor crouched beside him. He put a hand on his shoulder.

"I want to give Stafa a chance to play," Trevor said. "No point calling him up and keeping him on the sidelines."

"I get it," Cody said.

He didn't, really. The Lions had made it this far with their eleven players — the starting eleven.

"This can work," Trevor said. "You bring a lot of speed and energy to the midfield. And you can work with Kenneth and Paulo on the buildup to the attack. It's a change in mentality. You have to pay attention to defence, but stay aggressive and don't be afraid to join the attack when you see an opportunity."

Cody nodded.

"This isn't permanent. I'm trying stuff out. We'll see how it goes, okay?" Trevor said. He stood back up.

"You'll be fine. Go have some fun," Trevor said.

Cody got up. "Thanks, Coach. I will."

Ian's yelling interrupted them. "Ref, try watching the game and call some fouls. This game is turning into a joke," he screamed.

"Bad enough when he's managing the Storm. Now he has to watch our games?" Trevor said.

"Two teams are playing," Antonio's dad said. "Evens it out."

Trevor elbowed Cody. "We'll shut them up when we win this game."

"Sounds like a good idea, Coach," Cody said.

Trevor crossed his arms. "I know you're disappointed. This has nothing to do with your play. Stafa just doesn't have a midfielder's mindset. You can do this — and do it well."

Cody forced a smile. "It's all good. Seriously. I'm okay with it."

"I knew you would be," Trevor said. "Get out there. If you have open field, go for it. And if you have a clear shot, don't hesitate this time."

Cody took his spot on the field.

"Let's pick up the energy level, boys," Stafa said. He had the ball under his right foot. He nodded to Paulo. "We control the ball."

The whistle sounded. Stafa gave it to Jordan, who rolled it back to Cody. Cody found it weird to get a pass off a kickoff. It was the first time in his life, really.

A Flames forward made a beeline to Kenneth. The other forward marked Paulo. Jordan drifted left, a midfielder trailing him closely. That left Stafa wide open. A Flames forward was a few yards off. Cody hesitated only a half-second before passing to Stafa. Doubly weird that his first pass would be to the kid replacing him. The midfielder marking Jordan shifted over. Stafa had his back to him.

"Man on," Cody warned Stafa.

Stafa angled his left foot and calmly chipped the ball to Jordan.

"Nice play," Trevor yelled.

Jordan carried the ball over centre and then passed back to Stafa, who took it another ten feet before sending it square to Brandon on the left. Brandon approached the Flames back line carefully, then gave the ball to Paulo. Paulo simply one-timed it to Kenneth, inside, who in turn one-timed it to Stafa, camped out about five yards outside the box. Two Flames defenders converged on the ball.

"You're watching, Cody," Trevor said. "Get involved."

Cody wasn't a sure what to do. He'd always received the ball up front. It was different at midfield, in the middle of the action instead of close to the other team's defenders. The right sideline looked exposed. Cody pushed off and headed that way. Stafa guarded the ball with his body, drifting away from the Flames net. He looked up at Cody. Cody took the look to mean Stafa was going to pass. He began to sprint full-out. One of the central defenders took a few steps to get in Cody's way.

Stafa whirled and carried the ball through the gap made when the defender shifted to cover Cody. The other central defender tried to angle Stafa off the ball. But Stafa was charging like a bull and wouldn't be knocked off stride. Cody stopped running. The goalie came out, but before he could get close Stafa chipped the ball across the box to the right. Paulo ran onto it for the easy header.

A goal — just like that.

Cody watched Stafa as he ran in a slow, wide arc, his arms extended like airplane wings, head back. When Stafa got near the corner flag he jumped in the air, his right fist over his head. Benji and Ed came running down the sidelines, clapping. Cody coasted into the box, thinking, *A bit over the top.* Jordan had his arm around Paulo's shoulders. Kenneth held his hand out and Paulo gave it a slap.

Stafa leapt in between Jordan and Paulo. "I knew you'd be there," Stafa said. "I didn't even have to look. Just sensed it. You and me, bro, all the way."

Paulo held his hand down and Stafa gave it a slap. Cody felt like he'd been slapped in the face. One minute on the field and Stafa acted like he and Paulo had some special connection.

The Flames were already lining up. Cody hustled back to the right midfield spot — his spot now. He turned and faced the play. Good thing, because the Flames took a quick kickoff. The ball went to their right midfielder. A forward flew past Cody and the ball was lofted in his direction. Cody ran back frantically. The forward pushed him off with an arm. Cody leapt. The ball was falling a bit short.

"Use me," Stafa cried.

Cody strained to hold his position. The forward's shoulder banged into him. Cody craned his neck and met the ball with his forehead. Cody and the forward tumbled to the ground. A cheer went up immediately. Cody figured it was for a foul. He'd had position.

"Get off," the forward said to him.

"We call it soccer here. Save the tackles for football," Cody said.

Not the best comeback, but not bad under pressure.

Cody rolled away and got to one knee. That's when he noticed the ref hadn't blown the whistle. Maybe he was playing advantage, or maybe he didn't think it was a foul. In any event, Stafa, Paulo, Jordan, Kenneth, and Brandon were storming into the Flames end. Cody's header must've reached Stafa. Cody took off, but he was too far behind to offer support unless his teammates held it up.

Brandon gave the ball to Kenneth, who sent it to Paulo on the right. Paulo carried it inside and slid the ball to the right corner of the box. Stafa ran onto the ball and let it fly short-side. His quick shot fooled the goalie. Another goal. Cody couldn't believe it.

The goalie put his hands on his knees and lowered his head. The parents erupted in cheers. Kenneth, Paulo, Jordan, and Brandon threw their hands in the air. Stafa again ran in a wide arc to the corner flag and leapt in the air, fist held high.

Cody had to hand it to Stafa. Two touches — two goals. He'd blasted that ball into the top right corner, a beautiful strike. No hesitation. He did what Cody should've done at the end of the first half.

"That kid can play," Luca said from behind.

"Three – zip takes the pressure off," Cody said.

"Four – zip and we can start acting like superstars again," Luca said.

William joined them. "This is my favourite kind of game. Just sit back and watch the goals fly in."

"We've got to stay focused," Cody said. "One goal and they're back in it." He felt irritated but didn't know why.

"That Stafa is on fire," William said. "Keep feeding him."

"Nice header, Cody," Luca said.

He and William jogged forward to congratulate the goal scorer.

Cody stayed where he was. Two touches — two goals. *That kid could play.*

Nothing wrong with midfield. Lots of great players played there.

Only problem — Cody Dorsett was a striker.

Correction — he used to be a striker.

And if he wasn't a good midfielder, then who was he?

Cody finished his milk and put his knife and fork on the side of his plate. Kenneth had said after the Flames game that he might call about getting together to do something, like go to a movie. He hadn't. Not like it was a big deal. It was hardly the first time Cody would hang out at home for the night. His parents kept telling him he'd make friends at his new school in September. He wasn't the best at meeting people, though, and a new school was scary.

At his school back in Ferguson, he'd had a bunch of friends, guys he'd known since grade one.

"You've been quiet since the drive home from the game," his mom said. She softened her gaze. "Are you put out about moving from striker to midfield?"

"I don't know. A little, maybe." He shrugged. "It's been a long summer."

His dad put his fork down.

"I think we're still adjusting to moving here so we could be close to the hospital," his dad said. "You left all your friends and you haven't had the chance to go to school. So all you've been able to do is meet a few kids from soccer."

Were they reading his mind?

"Paulo's going home when the season ends," Cody said, "so that sucks too."

"I know we've been saying that once you go to school this September and you get to know kids here, you won't be so . . . lonely," his dad said. "But now your leg is so strong and you're playing soccer again. And, well, I've started my own business and can work from anywhere, really. Mom works from home, so —"

His mom jumped in. "We wondered if you wanted to move back to Ferguson, dear. We could even try and find a house in our old neighbourhood. You could go to your old school."

"It's just an idea," his dad said. "We're still thinking about it."

"I . . . We could go back, I guess . . . Maybe." Cody pushed his plate away. "It feels like we left a long time ago. Not sure where I feel more at home."

"It's only been a year," his mom said.

"I admit it feels long to me, too," his dad said.

"Everything keeps changing," Cody complained. "It's like . . . I get used to something and it goes away. I was this normal kid and then I have a lump in the back of my leg. The next thing I know we leave Ferguson and I'm living in a hospital and throwing up all the time."

51

His eyes began to sting.

"Cody . . ." his mom said gently.

"When do we have to decide?" Cody said.

"I guess in the next couple of weeks," his mom said. "That's if you want to start the year in your old school."

Cody slumped in his chair. "Not much time."

"No one said we have to go," his dad said. "Are any kids from your soccer team going to your new school?"

"No," Cody said bitterly.

"We didn't want to upset you," his mom said. "We are a little worried, though. Your life was disrupted. And with you going to high school next year, we want to settle down where you'll be happy, where you can make friends and have fun."

Cody put his hands between his knees and rubbed them back and forth. Paulo was leaving. He wouldn't see Kenneth or Luca until next season. And Mandy . . . Dumb to think of her. "I lost my spot on the Lions today, so . . . soccer probably isn't a big deal here," he said.

"You were still playing," his mom said. "It was only in the second half, and you played great in the first."

"I'm not sure Trevor agrees," Cody said. "Stafa plays Premier, not just Major. He's a year younger and he scored two goals. Trevor loves him. I don't know what's going to happen. Maybe I stay in the midfield?" He paused. "I'm a striker. Why do I have to move? Why does Jordan stay up? I have more goals than him."

"Sometimes we have to make changes for the good of the team," his mom said.

"I had to deal with Timothy and his stupid friends calling

me Egg-Head and Humpty," Cody said. "I've played hurt and I've worked as hard as I can at every practice and in every game." He sat up straight. "I know I'm whining. It's just that I'm tired of things changing 180 degrees every week." He hung his head.

"Like your father said, we don't have to decide right now," his mom said. "Think about it and we'll decide together."

Cody felt overwhelmed. Stay? Go? Did he really have a reason to stay?

The doorbell rang, interrupting his thoughts.

"Sean, you're not seriously meeting clients now? It's Saturday night," his mom said.

"Not me. I planned on spending quality time with my beloved family," his dad said.

The bell rang again. His parents looked at him.

"I'll get it," Cody said.

"Probably those kids selling garbage bags and plastic wrap to fundraise," his dad said.

"Do we need any?" Cody said.

"Not really, but I like helping them out. Get some medium freezer bags," his dad said.

"Gotcha," Cody said.

He went to the door and pulled it open. Kenneth and Luca peered in the door, with Paulo right behind them.

"Cancel your wild and crazy Saturday night plans, Cody," Kenneth said. "You've been summoned. Release the hounds."

"Why are we releasing hounds?" Luca said.

"What are we going to do with them?" Kenneth said.

"Let them go," Luca ordered.

"Who are you talking to?" Kenneth said.

"Who are *you* talking to?" Luca shot back.

They stared at each other.

"We're going to Talia's to watch a movie," Paulo said, over Kenneth's shoulder.

"Way to ruin the surprise, Mr. Surprise-Ruiner," Kenneth said.

"You weren't making much sense," Paulo said.

"When did she invite us?" Cody said.

"I got an emergency text around four . . . or five . . . or six," Kenneth said.

"So it was today," Luca said.

"Apparently," Kenneth said. "Mandy is driving her insane and she needs our company to mellow things out. Plus, she promised to make popcorn."

Mandy driving Talia insane? Talia and Mandy were best buds.

"Popcorn and a movie? What a terrible combination! We should pick up some salad," Luca said.

"I told her that," Kenneth said. "She said something about you being an idiot."

"I wonder what she meant," Luca said.

"I assumed she meant she doesn't have any dressing," Kenneth said.

"You two can shut up," Paulo said. "C'mon Cody. Let's go."

"Let me ask if it's okay," Cody said.

His mom had come over from the kitchen, her wallet in her hand.

"Hi, Cheryl," Kenneth said. "Can Cody have some salad while we watch a movie at Talia's?"

She raised an eyebrow. "I rarely understand anything you say, Kenneth," she said dryly.

"That's because Kenneth can't speak English," Luca said.

"What language does he speak?" Cheryl said.

"What did she say?" Kenneth said to Luca.

"She said we should go with salad, but only if we get Thousand Island dressing," Luca said.

"Obviously. It's not like we'd get ranch," Kenneth said.

"Talia invited us over," Cody said to his mom, "to watch a movie . . . and have popcorn . . . or salad."

"All right," Cheryl said. "Where does she live? I'll give you guys a lift."

"No worries," Kenneth said. "My dad's driving us." He thumbed over his shoulder.

As if on cue, his dad honked the horn.

"He gets scared when he's by himself in the car," Kenneth said. "Let's go."

"Have fun, boys," Cheryl said.

"Goodbye," they replied.

"What do you mean Mandy is driving Talia insane?" Cody asked Kenneth as they walked to the van.

Kenneth shrugged. "No clue. Just a text telling me to haul our butts over there, pronto."

Cody slipped into the back seat beside Luca. He realized that Mandy was driving him insane a bit too. What happened to her?

Talia's mom came to the door. She brushed her curly greyish-black hair from her face.

"Hi, Sharon," Kenneth said.

"Hello, boys," Sharon said. "Good to see you. Haven't spoken to you since we conquered City Hall and stopped the factory at Lake Tawson. How are the Lions doing?"

"We're in a fight for the playoffs. But as long as the boys give me the ball all the time we'll make it," Kenneth said.

"Oh, Kenneth," Sharon said. "You haven't changed."

Talia came up from the basement. She looked back down and yelled, "Mandy, the boys are here."

Cody heard footsteps. Mandy poked her head around the corner.

"Hi," she said.

Cody did a double take. At the lake, Mandy had worn a hat. Her hair, usually neatly tied in tight braids and gathered into a ponytail, was now dangling around her ears and the ends were all ratty. She wore oversized pants and a loose white T-shirt.

"We're making popcorn," Talia said. "You guys want butter, I assume?"

Kenneth, Luca, and Paulo started giggling.

Talia put a hand on her hip. "What's going on? You used to be almost mature — for boys."

Kenneth coughed into his hand. "Sorry. We didn't expect popcorn, not for a movie. It's a bit . . . weird."

Luca and Paulo broke up again. Cody didn't join in. He had been disappointed by the way Mandy was acting, but now he was worried about her. She looked tired, like she was sick.

"You head on downstairs," Sharon said. "It's popcorn, plus a few things. Could a couple of you give me a hand taking it down?"

"I'll do it," Mandy said glumly. She headed for the kitchen.

Talia's eyes opened wide. Sharon squeezed Talia's shoulder.

"I'll help," Cody said.

He wanted a chance to talk to Mandy alone.

Mandy was leaning against the counter by the sink. Cody took a few tentative steps in.

"How's it going?" he said.

"Just awesome," Mandy said.

He wasn't sure if she was being sarcastic. Probably not. She wasn't like that.

"Cool. How's the team going?"

Again, dumb thing to say. They'd talked about that yesterday.

She shrugged.

"What did you guys do today?" he said.

"Oh, we had tons of fun. We painted our nails and giggled and put makeup on and talked about what we were going to wear tomorrow."

That was definitely sarcastic.

"Right . . . um . . . What movie are we watching?"

"Don't know."

He figured he should come right out and say it. "I know you're . . . sorta . . . not happy about Paulo leaving. But we always knew he had to go back."

She crossed her arms. "I guess — since he lives in Brazil."

"I'm just saying, I get that you're sad about it and —"

"What are you even talking about?" she snapped.

He looked at her helplessly.

"You're suddenly talking to me and it's about Paulo going home?" she said.

"I'm not . . . What do you mean, suddenly? I just said that —"

"Heard you, Cody," she said sharply.

Forget sarcastic. This was plain mean.

"I'll take that tray down," Cody said.

He picked up a tray with fruit and a few cans of pop. "Not my fault Paulo's going," he said.

"Whatever."

This was a completely different person from the girl he'd told about his cancer. Or maybe this was the real

Mandy. He felt humiliated.

"Do what you want," he said. "I don't care."

"Thanks for your permission," she said.

He stormed out but hesitated at the stairs. He thought that maybe Mandy would call him back.

She didn't.

Everyone was sitting on a wraparound couch facing the TV. Sharon was standing by the bottom of the stairs, laughing with the others at Kenneth's story.

"I've missed you guys," Sharon said. "Talia's been so busy lately, and with Mandy here it's been exhausting."

"Excuse me," Cody said, turning sideways to get past her.

"Sorry, dear, let me take that from you," Sharon said.

"I can do it," Cody said.

"Cody, so thoughtful of you to cut up some fruit," Kenneth said.

"Such a nice job on the cantaloupe," Luca said.

Cody didn't respond. Why was it busy with Mandy there?

"Hey, Mandy. Do you have the popcorn?" Sharon called up the stairs.

"I'm going to bed," Mandy said. "I have a headache."

Talia's jaw dropped. "Mom?"

"It's okay," Sharon said. "She has a headache."

"She has lots of headaches. She gives me one too," Talia muttered.

"That's enough, Talia," Sharon said.

"The whole point of this was to —"

"I'll get the popcorn," Sharon said, cutting Talia off. "No

big deal. Start the movie." She went upstairs.

"What's with Mandy?" Kenneth said, uneasily. "She sick?"

"No . . . I mean . . . Yeah, she's not feeling too good lately. Mom thought a movie would cheer her up. Bad idea."

Talia's face had darkened.

"So . . . what movie should we watch, or have you picked one?" Paulo said.

"Please let it be about two people falling in love," Kenneth said, his hands cupping his chin.

"I think it's about machines that take over the world. Maybe someone falls in love," Talia said.

"As long as there's some love, I'm good," Kenneth said.

Talia reached for the computer. They waited quietly for the movie to start. "Here's the popcorn," Sharon sang out.

She put it next to the fruit platter.

But Sharon's voice sounded strained, Cody thought. And it was clear that Talia was bummed. So was he — the Lions, Stafa, Ferguson, Mandy. Life just wasn't going to let him be happy!

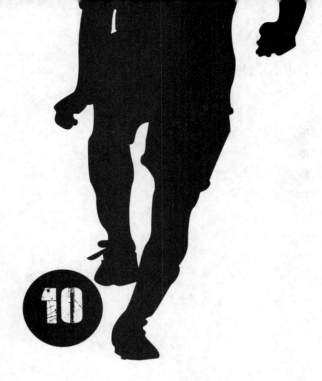

10

Cody hopped up on his toes, windmilling his arms. His legs were tight. He hated early-morning games. He felt like he'd just rolled out of bed. Everyone else seemed groggy, too. They were all on the sidelines putting on their cleats and taking off track suits and sweatshirts. It was unusually cold for an August morning. The wind was sharp, and the sky was dark and overcast.

"We need this game," Stafa said. He began rolling a ball between his feet. "Take a look. I printed out the standings."

He kicked the ball aside and reached into his bag to pull out a stack of papers. He handed them to Luca, who took one and passed it on. Cody was a bit startled by Stafa's boldness. The kid had played half a game with the Lions and he acted like he was the captain. Cody took a page and gave the stack to Ryan.

MAJOR DIVISION, as of August 12

		Games Played	Wins	Losses	Ties	Goals For	Goals Against	Points
1	UNITED	29	26	1	2	116	54	54
2	STORM	30	23	5	2	105	76	48
3	RANGERS	29	22	6	1	81	61	45
4	QUEENSLAND	28	20	8	0	92	81	40
5	SOUTH	29	15	10	4	81	70	34
6	LIONS	29	15	12	2	75	64	32
7	CLIPPERS	29	14	13	4	76	69	32
8	AFC	29	12	14	3	99	87	27
9	FLAMES	28	4	23	1	38	92	9
10	ROCKETS	30	3	27	0	19	128	6

"Gotta get fired up for this," Stafa continued. "We have to stay in the top six to make the playoffs, so this is a huge, huge game. We have three games to go, and if South wins their last three we won't catch them for fifth. AFC can still catch us, and they have a better goal differential, so we can't tie them. We have the Clippers on goal differential, but we face them in the last game of the season. It could come down to that. We got this, right, boys?"

He held out a hand to Jordan. They slapped.

Cody lowered his gaze. None of the guys seemed to care that Stafa was taking over.

"It starts today with AFC," Stafa continued. "They can score, but they also give up a lot of goals. We gave the Flames way too much time with the ball. Tons of pressure on the AFC defenders and they'll cough it up. And then we counter — hard."

Stafa slapped hands with Kenneth.

"We should have this game by half-time," David said.

"I've won the championship on every team I've ever played on. This team can win it too," Stafa said. "We've got way too much talent to be in sixth."

Cody tried to catch Kenneth's eye. He should be giving the pep talk, not some kid who'd been on the team for a few days.

"Let's get going with a warm-up," Trevor said.

Leandro kicked a few balls toward their goal. Cody began jogging over to retrieve one of the balls when Paulo called him over to where he was talking with Benji and Ed.

"Cody, can we have a quick chat?" Benji said.

"I've got to get ready," Paulo said. "Excuse me . . . and thanks." He gave Cody a serious look before heading out on the field.

"It's about next season," Benji said pleasantly. "Ed and me, we're putting together a new team — for the Premier league. We can't formally sign guys until the season is over. But we want to start evaluating the talent so we're ready. Teams in Premier are set by the middle of September. We don't have time to fool around."

"Trevor has told us a lot about you," Ed said. "We really like your game."

"You have good speed, you distribute the ball well, and you play with passion," Benji said. "That's a good combo."

Cody waited for them to continue. Were they inviting him to try out for a new team? But he was a Lion.

"Has Trevor spoken to you about next season?" Benji said.

Cody shook his head.

"We're recruiting the best players from Major to move up to Premier, like an all-star team. Ed and I will be coaching. We'd like to have you come out for a run this Wednesday, with some other guys."

"That Paulo, he's a sweet player," Ed said. "Too bad he won't be here."

"He lives in Brazil," Cody said.

"He told us." Benji laughed. "Too far to commute."

Cody smiled. He didn't feel like laughing.

"Anyway, we think you have the wheels and the work ethic. That's why we'd like to see how you stack up against the other guys we're inviting out," Benji said. "How does that sound to you?"

"Um . . . okay, I guess," Cody said. He wasn't sure how it sounded to him. He didn't want to be rude, though.

"Trevor was good enough to give us your parents' email. We'll send you the info for the practice. We've invited enough guys for a scrimmage," Benji said.

"Have a great game," Ed said.

Cody had somehow forgotten he had a game to play. "Thanks," he managed.

"By the way, Cody, we'd appreciate if you kept this very quiet. Just tell your parents. We don't want to hurt anyone's feelings, especially guys that we can't invite. So please, keep this under wraps, at least until after the season, when we can make formal offers."

"Does the league allow tryouts now?" Cody said.

"Not really." Benji grinned. "This isn't a *tryout*. It's a birthday party. Stafa's birthday was in July, so he's inviting a bunch of guys to play soccer to celebrate. It's like a birthday-party practice."

Sounded like a tryout to Cody.

"Don't worry, everyone does it," Ed said.

Benji leaned closer. "We're also speaking to Kenneth, your centre midfielder, and that goalie of yours . . ."

"David," Cody said.

"Yeah, that's him." Benji nodded emphatically. "Good luck today. Stafa's totally charged. Look for him all game. He's ready to dominate. I can tell when he's going to have a great game."

Cody had no idea what to say to that. "Do you want me to ask Kenneth and David to come over?"

"We spoke to them already," Benji said. "We'll be in touch, Cody."

He shook Cody's hand. Ed reached out and shook it as well, and Cody returned to the Lions end. The boys had divided into two groups to play keep-away. Stafa was firing shots at David. That was usually Cody's job — as the striker.

Cody joined Kenneth, Paulo, Luca, and William. Luca had the ball. He cut left and tried to slip the ball between William's feet, but the defender stopped it with his right heel. Paulo darted in and tried to strip the ball away, but William pushed him off with his arm to shield the ball.

"You're not allowed to use talent and quickness in soccer," Luca groaned. "That's a foul."

Cody waited for Kenneth to add a joke. Instead, Kenneth side-stepped over to him.

"Saw you talking to Benji and Ed," Kenneth said.

"A little."

"You . . . um . . . talk about soccer?" Kenneth grinned.

"I guess."

"Like . . . Premier talk?"

"Yeah."

"Pretty cool, huh?" Kenneth said.

Luca and Paulo hounded William for the ball.

"You guys playing?" Luca called to Kenneth and Cody.

Cody didn't want to talk about the Premier team, at least not now. It was just another thing for him to deal with, on top of everything else. The Lions were the one thing he thought wasn't changing, other than Paulo leaving. What about Kenneth and David? Did they want to play Premier? It sure sounded like Kenneth did.

Cody dashed forward and poked a toe between William's ankles. The ball bounced away. But he couldn't get around William, and Paulo got to it first. Cody gathered himself and slid over to mark Paulo. It was time for soccer. The Lions needed the win. He'd think about this Premier team thing later.

Cody prepared himself, the ball bouncing toward him fast. All the best players from the league were here for Stafa's birthday-party practice. He didn't want to look dumb by messing up in the warm-up. He jumped as high as he could. The ball hit him in the chest, but the spin sent it careening over his head. He whirled and trapped it with his right foot.

"Nice control, Cody," Benji shouted.

Cody sent a line drive across field to Marco, United's star player. The tall, broad-shouldered defender brought the ball down with his left foot, and in the next motion sent a rocket pass to one of his teammates.

"Feels bizarre to be on the same team with guys you're used to playing against," Kenneth said to Cody.

Cody looked around, then did a double take. "They

invited Antonio! I'm not playing with him. Every time we go up against the Storm he tries to take out my knees."

"Benji's picking the team," Kenneth said, "and he's friends with Trevor. He won't pick Antonio. Probably doesn't know what the guy's really like. He's a good player — even though he's a jerk," he added quickly.

David joined them. "Sweet birthday party." He grinned.

"It'll be fun," Kenneth said.

Cody looked around again. "I'm surprised they didn't invite Luca or William," he said.

A pained expression flitted across Kenneth's face. "Most of the defenders are from United . . . and I see a couple from the Rangers."

"They only invited twenty-two players from the entire league," David said.

"I think Luca and William deserve to be here," Cody said. "Jordan and Brandon, too."

The ball came to them. Kenneth stepped out and stopped it with his left foot. He passed the ball to a player Cody recognized from Queensland.

"That was a big win against AFC on Saturday," Kenneth said. "Those four goals will help with our goal differential. That Stafa is a machine — three goals." Suddenly, his face coloured. "And having you in the midfield, Cody, makes us ten times more dangerous on the attack, and more solid on D."

Cody didn't have a chance to respond.

"Check it out," David said. He nodded at the sidelines.

"Don't tell me Ian's going to be the manager," Cody said. "No way I'm playing now."

Kenneth cuffed his arm. "Let's find out what's up."

"They'll see us," Cody said. "We can't."

Kenneth flashed a grin. "We gotta get something from our bags . . . water . . . or something. C'mon."

The three boys sauntered casually to their backpacks. Ian was talking to Benji and Ed. Mitch stood a couple yards back.

"Hey, Benji, sorry we're late," Ian said.

Cody unzipped his bag and began rooting around.

Benji looked confused. "Late for . . .? Uh, Stafa's birthday just passed. He wanted to have a soccer party, so . . . We invited a few players from the league."

Ian laughed deeply and winked. "I've been around. I get it," he said. "I got no problem with it. José's never going to hear about this *birthday party* from me."

"I'm sure José would be okay with this," Benji said, tentatively.

"No worries." Ian laughed. "Besides, the rules are stupid. How are you going to put together a Premier team if you don't have a few tryouts? If you wait until after the season, all the best guys will be signed."

Cody could see that Ian wasn't acting like he usually did. He was being very friendly and had this dumb smile on his face. Cody also wondered who this José was.

"It's not a big deal," Ed said. "Just a little run around."

"For sure," Ian said. He looked at the field. "I see you've invited Antonio. Good defender. Plays hard. Not quite in Timmer's league, when you consider ball skills and all."

"Lots of talent around, for sure," Benji said.

Ian laughed. "I know the ropes. You can't sign players

yet. Don't worry. Like I said, I totally get it." He turned and waved toward the parking lot. "We should talk after practice. I have some ideas about sponsorship. I've got some contacts in England. Maybe the boys would like a trip over there to train in Manchester United's development program? I can make that happen."

Ian crossed his arms and his smile got even bigger. Cody looked over to the parking lot — and his heart sank. Timothy was running over.

Stafa broke off from a game of keep-away. "Are we going to get started?" he asked Benji.

"Give us a minute, Stafa," Benji said.

"Why's he here?" Stafa said, pointing at Timothy.

"Just give us a minute, please," Benji said, more firmly.

"I'll get the boys organized," Ed said. "It's no problem, Stafa. We'll clear this up."

Ed patted Stafa's shoulder and the two of them jogged back onto the field. When Ed blew his whistle, the boys stopped their warm-ups and headed to centre.

Cody and Kenneth's eyes met.

"If Timothy's playing . . ." Cody began.

Kenneth put a finger to his lips.

"You know Benji," Ian said to Timothy.

Timothy cocked his head back and nodded slightly. "For sure. You're Stafa's coach, in Premier."

"Awesome," Ian said. "Head on out, Timmer. And remember, it's just a birthday party."

Timothy grinned. "No problem. I got ya," he said. He dropped his bag to the ground and jogged to centre.

"So, let's definitely talk after practice," Ian said to Benji.

"Timothy obviously has to make the move to Premier. He's destroying Major. He is one of the top scorers, dominating every game. He needs the competition and . . ." Ian leaned forward and said in a quiet voice, "and I have the financial resources to help with things."

"Okay . . . I have to talk to the boys. We can chat later," Benji said.

"We should. I'm sure you don't want the Lions season to end badly," Ian said, in a suddenly serious tone.

Benji nodded uneasily. As he walked onto the field, Ian took out his phone and began poking at the screen.

Kenneth nodded to Cody. "Let's not worry about Timothy or Antonio. We've got this practice to deal with now," he said.

They joined the huddle of players.

Cody had half a mind to leave. The only reason he didn't was that it would make Timothy happy to see him go. No chance he was playing with Timothy — or Antonio. Or for Ian, if he was the sponsor or manager. No chance. He had no idea why Kenneth and David didn't seem to care.

Cody was content to stand at the back as Kenneth and David pushed their way forward. Timothy was standing next to Stafa. Timothy leaned over and whispered something to him. Timothy laughed. Stafa nodded his head a little.

Cody gritted his teeth and ground a heel into the ground. No matter what Kenneth said, he was going to worry about Timothy and Antonio — and Ian. This Egg-Head had put up with enough of their garbage to last a lifetime — even two lifetimes.

Cody watched as Marco ranged to his left with the ball. He and Cody were on the Red team. Marco sent it wide to his outside defender, who one-timed it to the left mid-fielder. Cody cut into the seam between two Blue players. The Red midfielder faked a pass to freeze the Blue players, and then he snapped a pass to Cody.

The pass was perfect. Cody turned up field. The Red centre midfielder broke free to his right. Cody gave it to him and continued forward. He was rewarded with a return pass. Cody snuck a glance to his left. Marco was powering his way up the side. That guy never stopped. Cody left-footed a pass over the Blue outside right back.

Marco ran onto it, stopping about twelve feet from the back line. The Blue defender watched him carefully.

"Not so fast, Dorsett," Kenneth said to him.

Kenneth was playing left midfield for Blue.

Stafa had shifted over to support Marco. Kenneth was a relentless defender. He wouldn't let Cody get open too easily. Cody needed to create space. Trevor had been on them for a couple of months about triangularity — three players creating triangle formations on the field. When it was done right, it meant two players couldn't take the ball away from the three players. By overloading a defence at speed, the attacking team created chances to go for goals. Cody had to get to Stafa and Marco to create a triangle before Kenneth could even the numbers out.

Cody took a step to his right, away from the ball. He pushed off from Kenneth ever so slightly to get him off balance, and then dashed back left. Marco and Stafa recognized the overload immediately. Marco passed to Stafa, who rolled it to Cody inside. Kenneth hustled to catch up, but he was still a step back. Cody sliced the ball with his left foot at the same time as Marco broke for the goal line. Stafa sprinted past Cody and Kenneth into the middle of the box. Cody's pass was perfect, and Marco roared in on net. The goalie came out to take away the angle.

Marco had no intention of taking a bad-angle shot. He took a few more steps and then cut the ball back into the box. Stafa slid hard, right foot extended, and redirected the ball into the wide-open net.

"Great support. Good ball movement, Red," Benji shouted. He blew his whistle. "Let's have everyone at centre."

Kenneth gave Cody a push from behind. "Ugh. Way to make me look bad," he said.

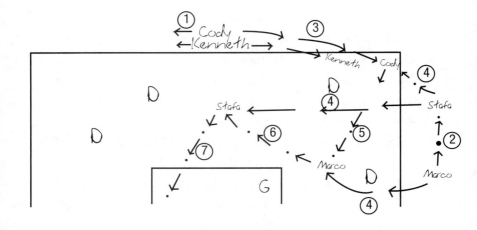

When he followed it with a laugh, Cody knew he wasn't serious.

"We gotta bring some of that in our next game against South," Stafa said. "We're four goals up on the Clippers, and our win over AFC means we're in if we win our last two games."

"Well done, boys," Marco said to Cody and Stafa.

"Good work on the wing," Cody said.

"Figured scrimmage was almost over, so why not. Gets dull defending all the time." Marco laughed.

"Just promise not to do that against us in the playoffs," Stafa said.

"Not sure I can do that. It was kinda fun up there," Marco said.

He and Stafa slapped hands.

"You United guys decide what you're going to do?" Stafa said.

Marco shrugged. "Obviously, we're interested. If the

guys on this field are in, I think it's a yes."

"I hope you guys play with us," Stafa said. "Benji and my dad have been planning this Premier team for a couple of years."

"When is Benji making offers?" Kenneth said.

"He can't until the regular season ends," Stafa said. "But I think he'll be talking to parents before then to figure out what guys want to do."

"Hopefully, we can all play together next season," Marco said.

The guys began to huddle around the coaches. Marco joined his United teammates.

"Awesome scrimmage," Benji said.

"Quiet down, boys," Ed called out, his hand over his head.

Kenneth elbowed Stafa. "Hear that? He said I was awesome."

"He meant everyone except you," Stafa said.

Kenneth looked up to the sky. "Why do I always get that wrong? I'm not awesome. I'm amazing. I can't make those kinds of mistakes in Premier."

Stafa laughed.

Timothy had edged his way next to Stafa.

"Thanks for inviting us to your birthday party, Stafa," Timothy said slyly.

"Yeah, no problem," Stafa said coldly.

Cody noticed that Timothy went a bit red in the face.

"I want to thank you all for coming out and working so hard," Benji said. "We wanted to give a bunch of you — the league all-stars — a chance to play together at least once."

"It won't be the last," Timothy said loudly.

The corners of Benji's mouth curled up ever so slightly. "Okay. So . . . There're twenty-three of you here. We can only have eighteen players next season. We have to talk things over, obviously. We'll be in touch no matter what. We want to be open and honest. It's competitive, though, and we need to take time to make the right decisions."

"We'll kick butt with the guys here, right, Stafa?" Timothy said.

"For sure," Stafa said slowly.

"We think this team has potential," Benji went on. "We're going to need to work very hard. We want soccer-obsessed kids who want to play more and more and more, players who have a hunger for the ball every second of every practice and every game. If you think that sounds like you, then maybe this is your team. Anyway, thanks again for coming out. You all did great."

Benji and Ed clapped their hands over this heads. A bunch of players let out a cheer.

"Hey, you guys wanna kick the ball around a bit more?" Stafa said to Kenneth and Cody.

"Sure, why not?" Kenneth said. "My dad loves waiting for me."

"Marco, you guys wanna knock it around?" Stafa called out. "Sounds good," Timothy said. "I'll play with Stafa." Stafa made a sour face. He chipped the ball toward the goal.

"David, you gonna play?" Kenneth said.

"Sorry, I gotta go," David said. "See you guys Friday. Go Lions!" He held his hand down low and slapped hands quickly with Kenneth, Stafa, and Cody.

"I have to go too," Cody said. He didn't really. He just didn't feel like hanging around.

"Okay, bros," Kenneth said. "Don't do anything stupid between now and Friday, like break a leg or forget how to play soccer."

Stafa jogged away to retrieve the ball he'd kicked.

"I can't promise the *not forgetting*, but I'll be careful with my legs," Cody said.

"You better. We need the Mailman at his best," Kenneth said.

"He's the Mailman now," Cody said, pointing at Stafa. "I'm more like the guy who takes the letters from the mailbox and sorts them . . ." His voice trailed off.

Least funny joke ever.

"Um . . . What are you talking about?" Kenneth said.

"Nothing, as usual," Cody said quickly. "Anyway, good practice. That was fun."

"It was cool. Every pass is right on the money and guys are always in position," Kenneth said. "We'll all make it. Benji said we were awesome!"

"Kenneth, heads up," Stafa yelled.

Kenneth took a few steps to his left and brought the ball down with his left foot. He whacked it back. Stafa headed it to Marco. Timothy bore down on him. Marco turned away and let Timothy take the ball. Timothy let out a whoop and then passed to Stafa.

"You and me, bro. Unstoppable," Timothy said to Stafa.

"I hope you guys realize we're going to have to kill Timothy if he makes the team," Kenneth said to his teammates.

"Count me in." David laughed. He nodded to the sidelines. David's dad nodded back. "Take it easy, guys." He jogged off.

"Sure you can't play for even five minutes?" Kenneth said. "I won't stay too long."

Cody really wanted to leave. "Can't. Sorry. My dad's here . . ."

"I forgive you," Kenneth said. "But next time you have to do whatever I say — and every time after that."

Kenneth began to play with Stafa, Timothy, and Marco and his United teammates. Cody walked to the sidelines. He didn't know how he felt about Premier. Big waste of time if he moved back to Ferguson.

He wasn't playing with Timothy and Antonio, or if Ian managed the team, not even if they trained with Manchester United, Chelsea, and Arsenal. But he had to admit that playing with guys like Marco would be sweet. It still wouldn't be like the Lions, though. Nothing would be. Premier was about winning. The Lions were about . . . the team.

13

"GO LIONS GO! GO LIONS GO!"

"A win today and we control our playoff lives," Stafa said over the sound of parents chanting and clapping.

Cody scuffed at the grass with his cleats. The boys were trying to psyche each other up. South was a solid team, probably better than their record indicated. The referee was talking to the sideline judges. The game would start soon.

"Let's go over our game plan again, while we have a couple of minutes," Trevor said. "Unfortunately, Leandro has to teach at the hospital today. He and I agree that South tends to come out a bit soft in the first half. We can exploit that."

"Don't forget they're in fifth and have us by four points. But if they lose their next two and we win ours, we have them on goal differential," Stafa said.

Stafa and Kenneth slapped hands. Luca's eyes narrowed as he watched them.

"That's generally the idea." Trevor grinned. "Luca and Ryan, I want you pressing up the sidelines every chance you get to give us flanking options. Cody, you need to be real active on the right side and play up even with Paulo. Ball goes to Cody or Paulo, and you two, with Kenneth, work it up the middle. Look wide to Luca and Ryan. Stafa, lots of energy, please, for the pass inside. We punch in a couple and then switch back to our usual 4-3-3."

"This is our game to win, Lions," Kenneth said.

"We better win it *this year*, Lions," Luca said. His voice had an edge Cody wasn't used to.

"We will win," Stafa said.

Luca shrugged. "I'm just saying next season is . . . whatever . . . Next season. Won't have the same guys."

Paulo said, "I won't be here, but —"

Luca cut Paulo off. "Guys are looking around, is all I'm saying. Next season will be different. We need to win this year . . . to win with this team."

Cody looked at Kenneth. Did he know about the birthday -party practice? Who told him?

Trevor cleared his throat. "There will always be changes in a team. Kids quit, move away, go to other teams. Nothing stays the same."

Luca held up his hand. "I'm not . . . No big deal. We should be talking about South, not next season. My bad."

Trevor's lips pressed together. "Luca's right. Concentrate on this game. Ultra-aggressive from the kickoff. David, be sharp and active in net. We'll be vulnerable to the counter-attack and may get caught short-handed."

David nodded and slapped his goalie gloves together. Most of the boys nodded. Luca didn't, and Cody noticed William seemed bothered by something too.

Tweet!

The referee was at centre holding the ball.

"Here we go, Lions," Stafa said. "Let's put our hands in."

Again, Cody was a bit shocked. Kenneth usually called for the team huddle. Sometimes Cody did it. He didn't think they wanted to hear from him now. He wasn't the striker anymore.

"Lions on three!" Kenneth yelled.

"One – two – three!"

"Roar!"

Cody was glad that at least it was Kenneth who called the cheer out. For a terrible moment, he thought Stafa would do that also. The boys began to drift onto the field. A hand tapped him on the shoulder.

"What are you thinking of doing next season?" Luca said to him.

"I . . . um . . ."

"Don't you think the Lions should stay together?" Luca said.

"Yeah — I guess."

Luca looked around quickly. "Did you hear about the practice?"

"The . . .?" Cody stood still, paralyzed.

"My dad found out from the father of a kid from the Rangers who was there," Luca said. "Stafa's coach, that

Benji guy, wants to put together a team next year, a Premier league team, with all the best players in our league." He leaned forward. "I think Kenneth was there . . . and supposedly a couple of other guys from the Lions."

Cody couldn't tell him now. It would be too weird after he had pretended not to know about it.

Tweet!

"Get in position, Lions," the referee said.

"Let's get this one," Luca said, and he backpedalled to his defender position.

Cody took his spot in a daze.

South had the kickoff. They played it back to their left midfielder. Jordan and Stafa pressured. The midfielder looked inside, but Cody sensed he would go the other way. Trevor had told him to be aggressive, so he took off to the sidelines. Sure enough, the midfielder faked a pass inside and snapped a pass to the South winger. He took the ball with his right foot, but his head was down, which is when Cody moved in.

Their feet smacked the ball at the same moment. But Cody had gone in harder, and he came away with it.

"Go, lads," Trevor urged. "Right at them."

The South centre midfielder cut across. Cody stepped over the ball with his left foot and did a spin, cradling the ball with his right. Then he sprinted into the open space, leaving the stumbling midfielder behind. The crowd cheered him on. The four defenders scurried to cover the field. Paulo fanned out to the right and Jordan had gone left. Stafa and Kenneth were storming down the middle.

Cody had lots of choices, but the best play was to Stafa.

Cody led Stafa by a few feet so he could run onto the ball. A South defender gambled and broke for it as well. Stafa flicked the ball on with his right toe. It rolled in between the central defenders. Stafa raced after it, with four Lions right behind. Stafa didn't seem to notice them. He took the ball straight in on net. The goalie bent low, arms wide, and angled downward. Stafa took a couple of stutter steps and then fired a shot to the left post.

The goalie didn't move, totally surprised by a kick from that distance. The ball grazed the inside post and went in.

"Goal!" a voice shouted — Kenneth's. Stafa spread his arms wide and curled in a wide arc to the corner flag. Benji and Ed were there, clapping and pointing at him. Stafa's father Gary stood behind them, arms crossed, a stern look on his face.

The Lions players arrived in a pack.

"Our one-man Strike Force scores again," Kenneth declared. He pushed Stafa in the chest.

"No letting up," Paulo said.

"It's Lions Roar time," Stafa said.

Stafa trotted back to centre, slapping hands along the way. Cody held his out dutifully.

"Nice intercept at the sidelines," Paulo said to Cody.

"Thanks."

Paulo hesitated. "We're a better team with Stafa," he said quietly.

Cody didn't answer right away. "You're right. It . . . feels different in midfield. I'm not used to getting the ball so far from goal. Everyone is around me now, and I don't know where to go half the time."

"You'll get it," Paulo said. He patted Cody's back and stopped at the kickoff circle. "But can you figure it out by the playoffs?"

Cody had to laugh. He flashed a thumbs-up. Paulo was right, though. He'd better figure it out — because the team was more important than where Cody wanted to play.

Cody was the Mailman and Stafa the Strike Force.

Strike Force was a better name.

Cody picked himself off the ground, weary but happy. When you're winning, the referee's whistle is a beautiful sound. It had just gone off.

3 – 2 for the Lions over South.

"That was too close for comfort," Cody said.

"I thought it was over when Stafa scored our first goal," Kenneth said.

"South got aggressive. They must've thought it was a real game for some reason," Paulo said.

"Lucky Cody got the third goal on Jordan's corner," Kenneth said.

"I didn't even see the ball. It hit my head and went in," Cody said. That was the truth. He'd jumped with another guy, and just able to get his head on the ball.

"We should've put it away early," Paulo said. "Trevor

won't be happy."

"We had to hang back to protect the lead," Paulo said.

"No worries," Kenneth said. "We won. Stafa's a force up front, and we're way more solid with Cody at midfield."

"I still feel bad for Austin," Cody said.

"Austin is a great guy and he doesn't complain, but he should be playing in a lower division. We all know that."

Luca stopped next to Cody. "Maybe it's that some guys want to play in a higher division," he said.

He continued to the sidelines.

Kenneth's face darkened. "I'm guessing someone blabbed about the birthday-party practice."

"I didn't tell him," Cody said.

"I get that some guys are mad they didn't get invited," Kenneth said.

"Luca's not like that," Cody said. "I think it's more about the Lions."

They joined the huddle around their coach. Luca was next to William.

"Relatively good game, lads," Trevor said. "Not sure our effort level was where it needed to be at all times. Solid start, obviously, but then we let them off the mat and back into the game."

"We gotta use this as motivation," Stafa said. "I take re- sponsibility for it. I totally didn't bring it today. Lost my edge. Maybe I thought we'd kill them after that first goal. I should've had at least three more goals. Won't happen again."

Cody couldn't get over Stafa's confidence. Reminded him of Timothy a little. They both thought they could score every time they touched the ball. The difference was that Timothy wanted to score so he could show off, so everyone would think he was the best player on the field. Stafa believed in himself too, but Cody could see that he wanted to score to help the team win. Stafa had taken Cody's position, and he was taking Kenneth's place as the Lions' leader — and for some reason, Cody still liked him.

"Last game of the season is Friday night against the Clippers," Trevor said. "I think we were looking past this game to that one. And we do need a huge effort. We win, we're in."

"Then we're in, because we're gonna win," Stafa said.

"Lions on three!" Kenneth cried.

"Roar!"

The cheer wasn't their best effort, like the game itself.

Cody was too worried about Kenneth and Luca to cheer. They were buds. That shouldn't end because of soccer. Like when Jordan and Brandon had stopped talking to each other earlier in the summer. They disagreed over the Marathon Game. The Lions had almost come unglued over that. Another feud could kill the team spirit — and just before the playoffs.

The guys drifted away to their parents, a few taking off their cleats first by the sidelines. Cody spotted his mom and dad talking to a small group of parents.

"Cod-y. Cod-y. Cod-y."

Cody laughed when he heard a girl's voice chanting his name. He went over to say hi.

"Hey, Mandy. Remember this guy?" Talia said cheerfully.

Mandy had been standing off to the side. She shuffled over, head down.

The good feeling Cody had from winning melted away.

"Nice game," Talia said.

"We take the next one on Friday and we're in the play-offs," Cody said.

"Woohoo!" Talia said. "We gotta come."

"I think we're busy," Mandy said flatly.

"What are *we* doing?" Talia said.

"Something other than watching soccer," Mandy said.

"I'm sure it can't compare with sitting in a bedroom staring at the ceiling," Talia said.

"Do what you want," Mandy said.

"Thanks for your permission," Talia said.

"Hi, girls," Kenneth said as he and Paulo walked up.

Talia took a deep breath. Mandy's face was dark and brooding. Kenneth looked at them uneasily.

"Um . . . didn't know you were watching," Kenneth said. "We would have sucked even more in the second half, just to entertain you."

"When do you play next?"

"Who cares," Mandy said.

"Mandy . . . So tired of this," Talia snapped.

"Then go sit in your bedroom and stare at the ceiling," Mandy said.

"Oh yes, that zany sense of humour again," Talia said, throwing her hands up in the air.

"Sorry for not being perfect," Mandy said.

"Like that's what I'm saying," Talia shot back.

"So leave me out of your plans from now on," Mandy said.

"Happy to," Talia said.

Mandy spun on her heel and walked away.

Talia breathed out. "Mandy!" Talia called to her. "C'mon. This is dumb. I'm sorry."

Mandy waved a hand over her head and kept going.

"Mandy, c'mon," Talia said.

Mandy began to run.

Talia closed her eyes for a moment. She opened them and smiled weakly. "Yeah, so . . . things aren't so good between us right now. Let's not talk about it."

"It's going around," Kenneth murmured. He glanced at the parking lot.

Cody followed his gaze. Luca was getting into his parents' car.

"What's up with you boys?" Talia said.

Kenneth paused. "Well, there's a new kid on the team. Stafa — the guy playing up front with Jordan."

"I wondered why Cody was in the midfield," Talia said.

"Stafa's a year younger. We're allowed to add him because he plays for the Lions team for his age group," Kenneth said. "Anyway, his coach wants to put together a Premier league team next season, our age, so Stafa will play a year up. He invited a few guys out for a birthday-party practice on Monday."

"And Luca wasn't invited?" Talia offered.

"Kenneth, me, and David went," Cody said. "Paulo was invited too, but he won't be here."

"Luca doesn't strike me as the jealous type," Talia said.

"I think it's more about the Lions breaking up," Cody said.

"Teams don't stay together forever," Talia said. "We have girls come and go all the time."

"Maybe it's also because they made us promise to keep it a secret," Cody said.

He was feeling awful about lying to Luca.

Kenneth nodded over Cody's shoulder. Cody turned around. His mom was there.

"Hi, guys," she said.

"Hi, Cheryl," they answered.

"Hi, Mom," Cody said. "Sorry . . . I thought you were talking."

"And I was, so no worries," she said.

"Did you like Cody's header?" Paulo said.

"Not sure if he headed the ball or the ball hit him." His mom laughed. "But I was sure glad it went in."

Cody liked that his mom knew her soccer.

"You all played very well," Cheryl said. "Good work."

"Thanks," Kenneth said. "The boys all rely on me in big games, since I'm the most talented and stuff."

Cody, Talia, and Paulo laughed. Cody had to force it. Kenneth's jokes didn't seem as funny without Luca to cut him down a bit.

"Why don't you all come over for lunch?" his mom said brightly. "I bought a ton of chicken on special. May as well barbecue it up."

Cody's chest tightened. His mom always embarrassed him, like he was a little kid and needed his mom to set up a play date. His friends didn't seem to mind.

"Sounds good," Kenneth said.

"Awesome," Paulo said.

"Thank you," Talia said.

"Wonderful," his mom said. "Come around twelve

thirty. Kenneth, can you ask Luca? And, Talia, can you get in touch with Mandy?"

Kenneth and Talia nodded. Neither looked too thrilled.

"I'm not really sure what Luca's doing," Kenneth said.

"And I don't know if I'll see Mandy," Talia said.

His mom shrugged. "Just let me know if they're coming. We have lots of food, like I said."

Cody's dad shook the car keys in the air.

"I have to drop Dad off downtown for a meeting. See you guys soon," his mom said.

Cody slung his bag over his shoulder. They said their goodbyes.

Cody hoped Mandy didn't come. She was acting weird lately, always angry for no reason. He got that she was bummed about Paulo. She was being a bit dramatic about it.

Maybe it was better if Luca didn't come either. Cody needed time to figure out how to tell Luca about the birthday-party practice, without it blowing up in his face, or affecting the Lions, or making things worse with Kenneth.

He had no idea how he would do that.

15

Cody's mom pointed to the chicken. "Cody, you're not eating much. Are you feeling okay?"

"I'm fine, Mom," he snapped. He knew how to eat. He just wasn't hungry. That thing with Mandy — her buzzing off like that — was really bugging him. So was the fact that things were more relaxed without Luca here.

The doorbell rang. Cody cast a worried look to the kitchen door. Was it Luca or Mandy? Cody could see that the others were thinking the same.

"I'll get it," his mom said.

"So, Cody tells me you're flying back to Brazil soon," his dad said to Paulo.

"Um . . . yeah," Paulo said. "Kinda sad — but excited about it, too. I can't wait to see all my friends and family. It's been four months."

"I guess it's back to school," Cody's dad said.

"I have a feeling you're right," Paulo pouted.

"Talia, do you know where Mandy is?"

Sharon had walked into the kitchen. Everyone sat up, shocked to see her.

"Mom? What are you doing here?" Talia said.

"Mandy's not home," Sharon said. "Do you boys know where she is? Cody, did she tell you?"

Why would she?

"Not really," Cody said. "I saw her at the game this morning . . . and she left."

Sharon turned to Talia. "What did you say to her?"

"Nothing. What do you mean?" Talia said.

"You told me Mandy left the game early to come home. Where is she?" Sharon said. She sounded panicky.

"I don't know. She was in her usual mood. She decided to walk home," Talia said.

Sharon looked at her watch. "It's two thirty, and she hasn't come home yet. And she won't answer her phone."

Talia's face clouded over.

"What happened, Talia?" Sharon said. "Tell me. It's important."

Talia hunched her shoulders and slouched back in her chair. "She was especially annoying this morning, Mom. You ask them. You can't even talk to her. I decided to go watch their soccer game and she came too. Then she spent the whole time sulking. I just needed an hour without having to deal with her."

"Talia — you know what she's going through," Sharon said.

"What about what I'm going through?" Talia said hotly. "She's impossible to be with. Seriously. She's so mean to me — to everybody."

"Sharon, what do you mean by 'what she's going through'?" Cody's mom said.

Cody listened intently. Was Mandy that upset over Paulo?

Talia sighed.

"Mandy doesn't want people to know," Sharon said. "But it's gotten out of control and I need your help to find her. The police say it's only been a few hours and she'll probably come home. They sent out a car to look for her, but there are only a few cars out on patrol right now."

"Why don't you sit," Cody's mom said to Sharon. "Would you like something to eat, or some tea or coffee?"

"No — thank you. I'm fine. I'm just so worried," Sharon said. She sat down. "I have a bad feeling. I think she's really upset and . . ." She put her hands on the table. "Mandy's been living with us the past few weeks. Her mom is not well."

Mandy's mom was sick? Why hadn't Mandy said something? Cody didn't know what to think.

"I hope it's not serious," Cody's mom said.

"Unfortunately, it is," Sharon said. "Mandy's been under a lot of stress, worried about her. I'm not blaming you, Talia. You've been amazing. Mandy's so vulnerable right now, so emotional. I don't think she's able to make good decisions." She closed her eyes for a moment. "We need to find Mandy. Where could she be?"

"Okay, we're going to help," his mom said. "Did the police say where they were going to look?"

"Not really," Sharon said. "They're driving around. They'll call the drop-in centre in town and check out the bus station and some youth hostels. I've called all the girls on Talia's soccer team and —"

"Oh, Mom, you didn't!" Talia said. "Mandy is gonna flip out."

"I'm flipped out, so she can join the club," Sharon said. She looked at her phone. "Hold on. The police just sent me a text." She read it. "Nothing. No sign of her. They want me to call back. Excuse me for a sec."

"You guys know her better than we do," Cody's dad said to the group of kids. "Where do you think she'd go?"

They all looked at Talia.

"I have no idea," she said.

"How about her school?" Cody's dad pressed.

"I guess," Talia said.

"Does she have any close friends?"

Talia breathed in. "Not really."

"How about relatives?"

"She has an uncle and aunt in Ferguson."

Sharon came back in. "The police are taking it more seriously now. They've contacted the police departments in the surrounding cities."

"Are they checking with her uncle and aunt?" Cody's dad said.

"I did already," Sharon said. "She hasn't called them."

"We won't find her sitting here," Cody's mom said. "Let's split up and start looking."

"We'll hit the streets on our bikes," Kenneth said.

"Does one of you have a phone?" Cheryl said.

Kenneth, Paulo, and Talia held theirs up.

"Call us every thirty minutes," she said.

"We'll call if we find anything," Cody said.

"Every thirty minutes," Cheryl said sternly.

"Mom, we can . . ."

"No problem," Kenneth said. "Let's roll. We'll hit City Hall first, and then spread out from there. I bet she went for a long walk."

Cody let it go. His mom was really upset, and he could understand why. A missing kid was a parent's worst nightmare.

"You should get a sweatshirt, Cody," his mom said. "It's a bit cool today."

"I'm fine. It's summer."

"Still . . ."

"I'm fine, Mom, seriously," he snapped. "C'mon, let's go."

Her eyes narrowed. Cody lowered his head and headed to the front door. She always pushed it, especially in front of his friends. He felt bad for being rude. He'd say sorry when they got back. A terrible thought occurred to him as he went to the garage to get his bike. What if Mandy's mom had cancer like Gavin? That would be beyond awful. Poor Mandy. Her brother dies, her parents divorce, the boy she likes moves back to Brazil, and then her mom gets cancer? No wonder she was messed.

Cody put his helmet on. He'd been mad at Mandy because she had a crush on Paulo instead of him. She could like who she wanted. He should've tried to help her, or at least asked if he could help. He hadn't done anything.

Not much of a friend.

He thought about Luca. Friends don't lie to each other, and Cody had lied to Luca about the birthday-party practice and the Premier team.

Not much of a friend at all.

Luca had a big heart, and Cody knew he'd be hurt when he heard they'd been searching for Mandy and hadn't asked him to help. He rolled his bike out of the garage.

"Wait one second," he called out. He ran back into the house and upstairs. He opened the laptop, clicked onto his Facebook page, and typed out a message.

> Luca, meet us at City Hall in ten minutes. Mandy is missing and we have to find her. No joke. Police have been called.

He hit Send.

Funny how simple life had been when he was getting his cancer treatments. He'd thought it was all about him, about Cody Dorsett.

He knew better now. It was never all about him, and he hadn't fought the cancer alone. He couldn't have made it without a lot of help, from his family, the doctors, the nurses — everyone. Mandy was trying to deal with all this alone, like a soccer player trying to dribble through the entire opposing team. That never worked.

Cody hoped he'd have the chance to tell her how sorry he was. He ran downstairs to rejoin the others.

Kenneth pulled up at the curb. Cody cruised in beside him.

"Does this girl have invisibility powers?" Kenneth said.

Luca stopped next to Cody.

"We've been everywhere — twice," he said.

Paulo and Talia circled around to face them.

"Mandy, I'm going to kill you when we find you," Talia yelled.

"Not sure she's going to hear that," Kenneth said.

"We've been riding around for five hours," Talia groaned. "What's with this girl? Where could she be?"

"You're her best friend. Can you think of anywhere she'd hang out? *Any*where?" Paulo said.

Talia hoped off her bike. "Everyone can stop saying that. I'm . . . like . . . It's getting on my nerves. I'm riding around feeling guilty, and I'm not even sure what I did wrong. Why is Mandy my responsibility? She's not my sister; she's on my soccer team. It's not my fault she doesn't have any friends. Our moms are friends and we hung out a lot as kids. But . . . she's not easy to be with, trust me."

"Sorry," Paulo said. "You guys are always together."

"Because I feel sorry for her, and my mom's always on me about including her in stuff. It was okay before Gavin got sick. Since then, she's lost it. I get that it was terrible, but still."

A gust of wind picked up, sending some leaves swirling around the street.

"It's not like she asked for any of this," Cody said.

"I didn't say that," Talia said. "I don't want to be a jerk about it. I just don't know what I'm supposed to do. Her brother died and her mom's in the hospital, and we're riding around the streets looking for her . . ."

Talia put her hand to her face and began to cry.

"I didn't mean it like that," Cody said. "I meant unless you've gone through it, you can't understand it."

Talia looked up at him.

"Cancer is like a huge wave coming at you. It's way too big to handle, like something that is going to crush you and wash you away. It's that way for the sick person and also for their family," Cody said. "I'm sure she doesn't mean to act like this. I bet she's embarrassed about it."

He took a moment to collect his thoughts.

"At least you tried," Cody continued. "I did nothing. And she and I went through the same thing, at least sort of, her brother and all. I was too into soccer . . . and myself. At least you tried."

No one said a word for a long time.

"I let her down," Talia said.

"You did your best," Kenneth said.

"I put up with her, but I didn't ask her how she felt. I brought her to places, and then complained about her to everyone. That's not what she needed." Talia wiped her eyes. "If I could just see her again I'd say sorry. And then I'd kill her for putting me through this."

"She couldn't have taken a bus or a train. The police checked," Luca said.

"It's too far to the next town to walk," Kenneth said. "Maybe she rode a bike?"

"Her bike is still at Talia's," Paulo said.

Cody had been thinking since they left his house. They'd checked out the school, City Hall Square, the ice cream shop, and the park. They even visited the girls on the soccer team who lived within walking distance. He had a nagging feeling they were missing something obvious. Where would she go when she felt bad, when she had no hope, when she was scared?

He couldn't believe how dumb he was.

"She's at Lake Tawson," Cody said.

"My mom told me she went there," Talia said.

"She didn't search hard enough," Cody said.

The others exchanged quick looks.

"That's a long ride," Paulo said.

"What time is it?" Talia said.

Kenneth looked at his phone. "Close to eight o'clock."

"I'm starving," Luca said. "I've gotta eat soon."

"We could grab a quick slice," Kenneth said.

Cody was tired and hungry too. He wished he'd eaten more at lunch. He hesitated and then said, "I'll go. No point in all of us riding to the lake. I'm probably being stupid. I have to look, so I'll know for sure."

A wave of emotion rushed over him and he struggled to hold back his tears. Mandy was alone. Scared. Confused. He'd felt like that when he was sick. He'd had his parents with him, though. Mandy probably felt like she had no one.

"Seriously, you guys grab something to eat. I'll go to the lake and look around," Cody said.

Luca pulled up on his handlebars. "I haven't been to the lake in a few days."

"I could use the exercise," Paulo said.

"The lake is beautiful at night," Kenneth said.

Talia got on her bike.

His friends weren't about to quit on Mandy.

"It's not your fault," Cody said to Talia. "Not Mandy's either. It's not anyone's fault."

Talia flushed. "I feel bad anyway — but thanks. Let's find her already, and . . . Let's just find her."

"I'm for that," Kenneth said. "To Lake Tawson!"

No one moved.

"That was kinda your signal to lead us there," Kenneth said to Cody.

Cody pointed a finger gun at him. "Just waiting for the right moment."

"This might be it," Luca said.

"Gotcha," Cody said.

Cody set off down the street, the others following in

single file. His butt was killing him after five hours of riding around. His legs were seizing up — and he was so hungry! He pushed the pain away. He stood up and began to pedal harder. He could be tired and hungry later.

"Yo, Cod-Monster, you're killing me," Kenneth called out.

"Keep up, old man," Cody said, over his shoulder.

"You're a bad person," Kenneth said.

Cody glanced back. They were all standing up and pedalling hard. Cody turned the corner and continued along to the street that led down the hill to the lake.

"Please be there, Mandy," he whispered under his breath.

17

Cody walked down the familiar forest path from the parking lot down to the water.

"It's going to get dark soon," Luca said.

"We better hustle," Talia said. "My mom sent me a text telling us to go back to Cody's."

Cody ignored them. He was going to find Mandy. He climbed a sand dune.

"She's not standing in the middle of the beach. We can rule that out," Luca said.

Kenneth and Paulo skidded down.

"Let's spread out," Cody said. "I'll go this way." He pointed left. "Maybe you guys can check out the other way."

He trotted down the dune and started walking along the beach close to the forest. Talia and Luca caught up with him. Cody looked back. Kenneth and Paulo were headed the other way. Cody sighed to himself. Kenneth and Luca had barely said two words to each other. Cody gave his head a shake. No time to worry about them. He looked into the forest. She had to be here.

For twenty minutes they searched.

"Cody, she's not here," Talia said. "I get why you think she'd come. This place is important to all of us."

Cody kept walking.

"Cody, we need to go back. It's getting dark," Talia said.

He clenched his fists. Talia grabbed his arm.

"Cody, seriously, looking here is not helping. This is wasting time," Talia said.

"Maybe," Cody said.

"Talia's right," Luca said.

Talia looked at her phone. "Another text. Everyone's at your house. They're ordering food in. I think the police are coming over too. They've issued a missing persons alert."

"This is out of control," Luca said.

Cody crossed his arms and slowly let his breath out. "Mandy loved this place, like me. We both feel safe here — healthy, happy. I thought for sure she'd come."

"She's not herself," Talia said. "I don't know what she's thinking. To be honest, I'm scared to know what she's thinking — or what she might do."

"We can't quit on her," Cody said, fighting a sense of desperation.

"Let's not start feeling bad again," Talia said. "This isn't our fault."

Their eyes met. He could tell she didn't believe that, and neither did he.

"I bet Kenneth and Paulo are coming back," Luca said.

Cody let his head drop. "Okay. Let's go."

Talia and Luca led the way. Cody kicked at the sand. He looked out on Lake Tawson. The sun had set, and the darkness was spreading across the beach. The water was still, barely moving, just thin ripples edging up the shore. He wished he was as calm as the water. His heart was racing and his chest felt tight. Where could Mandy be? He'd been so sure. Riding over, he'd pictured Sharon and Talia yelling at Mandy and then giving her big hugs. Talia and Mandy would make up — and things would be back to normal.

He didn't really know what normal was anymore.

Cody watched Talia and Luca up ahead. He picked up some sand and threw it into the forest. He wanted to scream. He'd dragged them all here. They'd be mad at him. He picked up some more sand and let it fall between his fingers. He heard some branches crackle in the forest. Must be a squirrel or something. Once, he'd seen a fox down here, a little brown one. He looked closely. He saw something brown. He tiptoed closer. A few twigs cracked and he stopped. He bent down. It was still there.

"Yo, Cody. You coming?"

"Thanks, Luca," Cody muttered. The fox, or whatever it was, would run off. He took a quick look. It was still there. It couldn't be an animal. Luca's shout would've scared off an elephant. He crept closer. Behind a bush he could see something long and brown. He took a few more nervous steps. It was way too big to be a fox. He craned his neck around the bush.

"Mandy?"

She sat up, her eyes dazed, looking around wildly.

"Mandy, it's me, Cody."

He rushed next to her and dropped to his knees. She'd been covered up by a brown blanket, using her backpack as a makeshift pillow. Mandy pulled her legs into her chest and wrapped her arms around her legs tightly.

"We've been looking for you for hours. Talia, Luca, Paulo, Kenneth, me, and my parents and Sharon, and everyone else's parents . . ." Cody started.

She was crying

He sat back on his heels. "We're all real sorry — about your mom. It must be —"

"Nothing I can do about it," she said bitterly. "Dad's gone, Mom's cracked up, and I'm lying in the forest, a homeless person."

"You're not homeless," Cody said.

What did she mean by *Mom's cracked up*?

"Then where do I live?" she said.

"You're at . . . Talia's right now," he stammered.

"They hate me and I don't blame them. I'm driving Talia crazy, and Sharon too. They want me gone," Mandy said.

"That's not true," Cody said. "Sharon is totally worried and Talia feels bad about . . . She's been looking for you for five hours."

"I saw her. Sharon, I mean, walking along the beach," Mandy said wearily. "I didn't know what to do — or say — so I kept hidden in the forest and she left. Stupid, but it never occurred to me that she was looking for me. Just thought she was going for a walk."

She shook her head angrily. "Anyway, my dad left to

work in New York City, said he needed a change. Translation, he wants to get away from me and Mom. When my mom went to the hospital, I moved in with Talia."

"Talia wants you to come back. She's sorry for the argument after our game. She really is," Cody said.

"You don't really get it, Cody. My mom's asking too much. Sharon isn't my mother and Talia's not my sister. They don't have to take care of me. Obviously, my dad doesn't want to and my mom can't."

"When did your mom get sick? It's not . . ." He swallowed heavily. "It's not cancer, is it?" Cody said.

"No. It's not her body. It's here — in the head," Mandy said. She pointed at her temple.

Cody waited for her to explain.

"Mom has depression, and now she's in the hospital," Mandy said. A short sob escaped her. "I've been so impossible lately. And I've been mean to you. I'm sorry."

"You don't have to apologize," Cody said. "I should be the one saying sorry. I should've asked what was wrong instead of getting angry and . . . being all sensitive about my feelings."

"You're allowed to have feelings," Mandy said. The slightest of smiles appeared on her face.

He picked up a twig. "I was . . . This is going to sound really, really dumb, but . . . I thought you were messed up about Paulo leaving. I thought that's why you didn't answer my messages — and you looked kinda upset at the lake that day." His face had grown hot. He snapped the twig in half and tossed it aside.

"I wanted to answer your messages," Mandy said. "I read

107

them. I was . . . It was around the time my mom was having trouble. I was stressed out about her and worried and . . . Then she went to the hospital. And then I didn't want to talk to anyone. I was so messed when we met at the lake and . . . I got sad seeing everyone together. I was scared you'd all be freaked out about my mom."

"My bad, totally," Cody said quickly. "I took it the wrong way. I was being dumb."

"You weren't being dumb. Well, maybe a bit, about Paulo."

His face got hotter.

"I'm sorry he's going, but it's not like that. He's just a friend," she ended in a rush.

For a moment, Cody felt happy inside, almost giddy. Then he remembered about her mom.

"I like your mom, and I'm sorry she's not feeling well," Cody said. "It must be really hard for her, first with Gavin and then your dad . . . My mom went a little —"

He had almost said "crazy."

"She had a hard time dealing with me getting sick," Cody continued. "I think she still does, which is why she's so worried about me all the time. I think I've been mean to her, losing my temper and telling her to leave me alone. She's trying her best, which is more than I've been doing."

"You're too hard on yourself," she said.

He looked away. "How is she? Your mom, I mean."

"Not sure. Better, I guess."

"When was the last time you saw her?"

"Couple weeks ago."

"Mandy?"

"What do you say to your mother when she's crying all the time or can't get out of bed? She's gone nuts," she said. "I can't visit her. She's crazy. It'll make me crazy."

"Don't say that," Cody said. "She's . . . sad, obviously. And it's okay to be in a hospital to get better. I was in a hospital."

"Not for your brain," she said.

"People get sick in lots of ways," Cody said.

"That's so true for my family," Mandy said.

"I can't pretend to understand how you feel," Cody said. "But I wanted to say I'm sorry for not being a better friend. I didn't think about things from your point of view. I was too into my stuff." He took a deep breath. She was crying again.

"Where were you going?" he said.

She threw her hands up. "Good plan, huh? I was so angry, I ran to my house, grabbed some extra clothes and a blanket, and took off. I wandered around for a while, and then . . . ended up here." She slapped the ground. "I'm so embarrassed. I can't go back to Talia's, not after this."

"You can," Cody said. "A lot of people want to help you. We let you down by not asking what was wrong, and you let us down by not asking for help. I promise there's no problem going back to Talia's. And when your mom is better, you'll go back to your real home."

"How do you know my mom will get better?"

Her question hung in the air until the sound of the others running up chased it away.

"Mandy!" Talia exclaimed.

"I'm sorry, Talia," Mandy said, bursting into tears.

"Shut up," Talia said.

Both girls were crying and hugging each other.

Kenneth, Paulo, and Luca looked on awkwardly.

"We should tell Sharon we found her. The police will want to know," Luca said finally.

Talia took out her phone. "We'll talk about all this later," she said to Mandy. "How about we get home and have something to eat?"

"Okay," Mandy murmured.

Talia tapped out a quick text and shoved her phone into her pocket.

"I don't have a bike," Mandy said.

"I'll double you," Cody said.

Mandy bundled her things into her backpack. Cody wanted to ask Mandy a thousand questions, and he guessed the others did as well. But they didn't say a word, not on the way to the sand dune, up the path to the parking lot, or riding back to Cody's house.

18

Cody yawned and he rubbed his eyes with his fingers. He needed to snap out of it. He felt like he hadn't slept at all. It was already late by the time they'd come home after finding Mandy. Then they ate and talked for a while. Then he stayed up talking with his mom and dad about mental illness and depression. His mom said that depression was a disease and not Candice's fault. She also said that people could get better and usually did.

When he finally lay down, his brain went into overdrive. He couldn't stop thinking about having lied to Luca. Finally, Cody realized he wouldn't sleep until he did something about it. He got out of bed and sent Luca a message to meet him. For some strange reason he said he could come over at nine thirty in the morning — and so here he was, in front of Luca's house.

"Do it already, Dorsett," he murmured.

He went to the front door and knocked. It flung open.

"Hey. Saw you waiting on the sidewalk," Luca said. "Why were you just standing there? Were you on the phone? I thought you were the last kid on the planet without one."

"No . . . just trying to wake up, I guess. Still no phone."

Cody felt like he was in math class before a big test. His stomach fluttered and his heart was beating faster than normal.

"Come on in," Luca said.

"Sure, thanks." He came in. "You were up late last night," Cody said.

Luca had answered his message right away.

Luca ducked his head and nodded. "I couldn't sleep. Thinking about stuff, I guess."

Cody stepped into the hallway. The house was small, but neat as a pin. The first floor was one big room. The kitchen was at the back, with a table in the middle, and a couch and chair at the front. A TV was hanging on a wall. Luca's mom was standing in front of an island counter in the kitchen part.

"Let's go downstairs," Luca said.

Luca's mom put down a bowl and walked over. "Hi, Cody. Nice to see you."

"Hi, Jeannie," Cody said. "How are you?"

"I'm quite well, thank you," she said. "How is that poor girl, Mandy? Luca told me all about it. So sad. Thank goodness you kids found her. She must have been terrified. I'm so proud of you all."

"Cody found her," Luca said.

"We all did," Cody said quickly.

"Doesn't matter," Jeannie said. "Hopefully, her mom gets better and Mandy can get some stability in her life. Cody, do you want something to eat? We're eating breakfast in about ten minutes. I'm making banana bread."

"I wondered what smelled so good," Cody said. "But I ate, thanks."

"He'll have some, Mom. He's being polite," Luca said.

"I figured." She laughed. "I'll call you when it's ready."

Cody followed Luca downstairs.

"So, are you playing with the Lions next season or what?" Luca grinned as he sat down.

Cody sat across from him. "I'm that obvious?" he said.

"I know that Benji is putting a new team together. Stafa will be on it, and maybe some guys from the Lions, like maybe Kenneth, David . . . you?"

"Who told you?"

"Hard to keep a practice with twenty-two guys from the league completely secret."

"It guess it was stupid to think no one knew."

Luca lowered his brow. "Bro, c'mon. It would be tough to raid other Premier teams. Most guys stay where they are. Benji has to poach players from Major, an all-star team of kids who want to move up. You three are our best players. It only makes sense. Paulo's leaving or he'd have been out there too, I bet."

"He was invited," Cody admitted.

Luca pushed back into the corner of the couch.

Cody gripped the armrests. "It's sorta like you said.

Benji and Ed invited me to this practice. They called it a party, like it was Stafa's birthday, so it wasn't breaking any league rules."

"Everyone does that," Luca said. "You can't sign guys until the season ends, so you pretend it's a birthday party and have tryouts. If you wait too long after the season, all the good players are signed with other teams."

"Benji asked me to the practice, and I went. He made it seem important, like I was being invited to some big thing."

"What was the practice like?"

"We scrimmaged, mostly. There were two full teams. Plus Timothy, uninvited."

Luca's eyes bugged out. "You're kidding. He just showed up?"

"Ian was all buddy-buddy with Benji and offered to sponsor the team. Antonio was there too, but he was in-vited. No way I'm playing with Timothy — or Antonio. Or for a team Ian has anything to do with."

"What if Timothy and Antonio don't make it? Will you play?"

Cody slumped back in his chair. "I wanted to say sorry about not telling you about the practice when you asked. Benji said it was a secret and . . . I was being dumb. I should've told you. Sorry."

"It's cool. I get it. You should play, though. Premier is big time, and you can totally make it."

"You could too, and a few other guys on our team."

Luca looked away. "Not sure. I like playing on this team — or what's left of it. You figure Kenneth's playing?"

"Not sure. He didn't say."

Luca looked at him.

"But probably, if they ask him," Cody said.

Luca didn't respond right away. "It's not that he shouldn't if he can make it. That's up to him. But to not tell me, or anyone, like it's some big secret? That's not cool. We're a team, or at least I thought we were."

"We *are* a team," Cody said. "No one's leaving until the season's over."

"Then that's it? We had to suffer through Ian and Mitch, and Timothy and his jerk friends, and play with only eleven guys? Not to mention the Marathon Game. After all that, guys just quit?"

"We're not quitting on the Lions," Cody said. "I haven't made up my mind. And like I said, I'm not playing with Timothy or Antonio. I haven't been asked yet, either."

"You will."

"Maybe."

Luca put his feet up. "What do you think is gonna happen?"

"The Lions stick together or fall apart. It's our choice," Cody said.

Luca laughed. "I meant with Mandy."

Cody had thought about her a lot last night too. "Hard to say. Like your mom said, hopefully Candice gets better and Mandy can go home. Her dad sounds like a jerk, running off to New York. It's brutal."

"Boys, the banana bread is ready," Jeannie called down.

"No matter what happens, though, Mandy needs to stop feeling sorry for herself. And she needs to help her mom," Cody said.

"It's getting cold," Jeannie added.

"We're coming, Mom," Luca said. He hopped off the couch. "Let's drown our troubles in warm banana bread and butter."

"Swimming in banana bread makes no sense, but I think we should try it anyway," Cody said.

Luca stopped in front of the stairs. "Sometimes I think you might actually have a sense of humour." He flicked his eyebrows and continued upstairs.

Cody slapped the armrests and got up. "Trust me, I'm hysterical," he called out.

He heard Luca laughing. Cody smiled to himself and went upstairs too. He felt that warm feeling you get when you've done the right thing. By the top of the stairs that feeling was gone. He wasn't finished yet.

He had one more thing to do. But first, banana bread.

Talia and Mandy turned at the same time, both obviously startled to see Cody. He'd come straight over to Talia's house after leaving Luca's. Talia hit the space bar to pause the movie playing on the laptop. She was still in her pyjamas. Mandy wore baggy shorts and a T-shirt.

Cody pointed at Mandy. "You and I are going for a walk."

Talia giggled.

"And where are we going?" Mandy said, her eyebrows arched.

"That's a surprise. But you don't have a choice, so come on," Cody said.

Cody knew he was making a fool of himself, but he didn't care. This had to happen.

"Get going, Mandy," Talia said, smiling. She tapped the

space bar again to start the movie.

"You're coming too," Mandy said.

Talia shook her head. "You heard the boy. You have to go. I have a choice."

For a moment Mandy's eyes hardened. "I guess a walk wouldn't kill me," she said, and she got up. "Where to again?"

"I told you. It's a —"

"Yeah, yeah. It's a surprise," Mandy said. She rolled her eyes, her lips curled in a slight smile.

The fifteen-minute bus ride passed quickly enough. They didn't talk about anything important, mostly soccer. Cody figured Mandy had had enough heavy conversations lately. Besides, things were about to get really heavy soon enough. The bus stopped at a corner and they got off. Cody gave Mandy a cheesy smile.

"Surprise!" he announced.

"You're kinda losing me here," Mandy said.

Cody nodded down the street to a large, mostly white, brick building. Out front, in large blue letters planted in the ground, was the word HOSPITAL.

"This isn't happening, Cody," Mandy hissed.

"I don't always face my problems," Cody said, as if she hadn't said a thing.

"I'm not asking you to get involved," she said. "I'm not asking you for anything."

Cody could see she was seriously mad. He reminded himself that she needed him to be her friend. And that sometimes friendships got messy. He forced himself to go on.

"I'm real good at ignoring how I feel, trust me, and worse, worrying about what other people think of me," Cody said, "especially when my hair had fallen out. I couldn't stop thinking about it, obsessing about it. I always wore a hat, and I thought every person in the world was staring at me. They weren't, of course, and I let guys bully me over nothing. I should've just said, 'Yeah, bro, my hair fell out because I took medicine to kill the cancer in my leg. Deal with it.' Instead, I almost quit the Lions like a big baby."

"That's different," Mandy said. "You were sick. That's nothing to be embarrassed about."

"Your mom is sick too. She has depression. It's a disease. It's the same as cancer."

"Hardly," she said angrily. "With cancer, you aren't crying all the time and staring at pictures of Gavin like he's going to magically come back to life."

Tears fell down her cheeks. Her fists were clenched tightly.

Cody took a step forward and touched her shoulder gently. She didn't move away. He rubbed her shoulder, and then pulled her closer and gave her a hug. They'd danced together once, on the beach, to celebrate after the Marathon Game. He'd been all nerves then, worried he would do or say something dumb to ruin the moment. This was different. It felt right.

"I get the embarrassed part," he said, letting her go. She rubbed her eyes. "But I don't agree that she's that different from me. We both needed to be in a hospital to get better. And if people have a problem with that . . . well . . . they can stuff it. At least, that's how I feel."

Mandy crossed her arms tightly. She didn't say a word.

"I figured you needed a friend to drag you here. You know your mom wants you to visit. She does. So . . . let's visit." He held out his hand.

Mandy took a deep breath.

Cody smiled and held his hand out again.

Mandy stretched her arms wide, and then, with a sigh, took his hand in hers. Her hand felt a little cold at first, but it warmed up by the time they walked into the hospital. They went to the information desk.

"I'm . . . uh . . . wondering if you can tell me the room number for Candice . . ." Cody suddenly realized he didn't know Mandy's last name.

"Knoll," Mandy piped up. "Candice Knoll."

The man looked at the computer screen.

"Are you family?"

"She is," Cody said. "Her daughter."

"And you?" the man said.

"A friend," Cody said firmly.

"Okay, she's on the fifth floor." The man looked at Cody. "Not sure you'll be allowed to see her."

"That's fine," Cody said.

The man looked back at the screen. "Elevators are over there, to your right," he said.

"I was on the third floor," Cody said quietly as they waited for the elevator.

Mandy's eyes had gotten red and puffy, and her face had lost its colour.

"You'll be fine," Cody said. "You're just going to talk to you mom, like you've done a million times."

Mandy said nothing. They entered the elevator, rode up in silence, and then got out at the fifth floor.

"It's here to the left," Cody said.

"How do you know that?" she said.

"I used to get so bored sitting in my room I'd walk the halls for hours. It was actually fun late at night when it was real quiet. They dim the lights and it's almost spooky. It kept me from thinking about the next treatment."

They pushed through a pair of doors.

"I feel sick to my stomach," Mandy said suddenly.

He put a hand on her back. "C'mon," he whispered, pushing her along.

She didn't resist.

"Excuse me," Cody said to a nurse behind a desk. "We were told to come here to visit Candice Knoll? This is her daughter, Mandy. I'm a friend."

The nurse smiled. "You're Mandy? Wonderful. Absolutely. Let me check where she is. She went down to the cafeteria earlier."

"She's allowed to do that?" Mandy said.

The nurse laughed. "Of course. She can go where she wants." She picked up the phone and spoke briefly. "Well, you're in luck. She's reading, in the lounge. You can go on back. It's around the corner."

"I'll wait for you here," Cody said. "Take as long as you want."

Mandy took his hand without asking. "You're coming with me," she said.

It wasn't a request. Cody let himself be dragged along. Mandy squeezed his hand harder with each step.

"Mandy? You're sort of crushing my hand," he said.

"Sorry."

"No worries. Try to take it easy. She's your mom."

They turned the corner. Cody almost gasped out loud. This wasn't the Candice he knew from just a few weeks before. That woman had been bursting with energy. Her hair had been jet black with tight curls, her eyes bright and intense. This Candice sat in a chair, a book in her lap. Her face was drawn and tight. A scarf covered her head, with tufts of frizzy hair peeking out. She seemed smaller, like she'd shrunk.

"Hi, Mom. Sorry I didn't visit before. Soccer's been really busy . . ." Mandy's voice trailed off.

Candice got up slowly.

"Maybe I should go back to the desk," Cody whispered to Mandy.

"No," she answered.

"It's okay," Candice said.

She sounded tired, like she'd woken up from a deep sleep.

"How are you, M?" Candice said. "I've been speaking to Sharon most days. She said things were good. Having fun with Talia, I bet, like one big sleepover."

Mandy clasped her hands behind her back. "It's okay, Mom. Maybe not exactly like a sleepover."

"Of course not," Candice cut in. "I'm being silly."

"It's been fun, sure. I . . . um . . . I've been sort of worried about you, though, a lot . . . And sometimes . . . maybe . . . I've been giving Talia a hard time. I've been a bit of a jerk."

"Don't be too hard on yourself. This is a struggle for everyone, and I'm sorry for this."

"Um . . . how are you feeling?"

"I think I'm much better, M. They're taking good care of me here."

"Good. That's good. I . . ." A sob caught in Mandy's throat. "I'm sorry for not coming. I've been —" She broke off and looked over to Cody helplessly.

"We've both been playing a lot of soccer," Cody said. He figured she needed him to do some talking. "Mandy's team is doing awesome. They're in first. Playoffs start next weekend — Championship Weekend, which is what they call it. I think Mandy is second in scoring in the league, behind Talia. And Mandy's a midfielder, so . . . that's cool. We find out if my team makes it tomorrow. We have our last game of the season. If we win, we're in."

He left off. Mandy and her mother weren't listening.

"Give me a hug, M. I've missed you," Candice said.

Mandy crossed her arms and clasped her elbows, head bowed.

"I know this is unpleasant . . . and embarrassing," Candice said. "I could just really use a hug."

"I need to . . . make a call," Cody said. "Excuse me. I'll . . . be right back."

Mandy took a step forward, hesitated, and then ran to her mom. Cody took a quick glance back. Mandy's head rested on her mom's shoulder, her shoulders shaking slightly while her mom stroked her head.

Jordan took a pass from Kenneth, about fifteen yards from the box on the right side. He faked an outside move and tried to dribble past the Clippers outside left defender. The defender turned sideways and threw his left hip into Jordan's right leg. Jordan fell and the ball bounced to the Clippers left midfielder.

Stafa, Kenneth, and Paulo stopped running. Ryan had been charging up to join the play and he bent over to catch his breath. Cody began walking. Good time for a free kick. The game was tied 1 – 1 deep in the second half. The Clippers had the goal differential. A tie and they would make the playoffs instead of the Lions.

The Clippers midfielder took off with the ball toward the Lions end. Cody hesitated. The whistle hadn't gone.

"Where's the foul?" Cody yelled. He began to give

chase. The referee was running up the field. No foul! A Clippers goal now would be a disaster.

The Clippers midfielder punched the ball forward about twenty yards downfield. A Clippers forward ran onto it, with four teammates in support. He gathered the ball and carried on down the right side. Then he slowed, as if getting ready to cross it. Cody took a huge stride and dove, right foot extended. The winger swung his foot.

Thud!

The ball smacked Cody's shin and bounced out of bounds. His leg stung, but it also felt good. That could've led to a goal if the cross had gone into the box.

"Awesome play, Cody," Talia cheered.

He got to his feet. Mandy flashed him a thumbs-up. He nodded back, and then he shifted over to mark a player and prevent the quick throw-in. Luca and William also marked Clippers forwards.

Kenneth arrived next. Cody expected him to say something to fire them up. Kenneth stayed quiet and took a spot behind a Clippers midfielder.

The throw went back to the Clippers left midfielder, who gave it to the closest defender. Stafa anticipated the pass and ran at him. The defender turned around and stuck his hip out. Stafa bounced off the bigger player. The defender snapped a pass inside. Stafa slapped the sides of his legs.

"Keep at it, Stafa," Benji called from the sidelines.

"Another foul, ref," Ed said.

The ball returned to the Clippers outside defender. Again, Stafa went at him. Again, the defender used his big frame to keep Stafa away. The defender suddenly whirled to the outside, swinging his right elbow into Stafa's stomach. Stafa bent over and put his hands across his ribs.

"That's such an obvious foul!" Ed yelled.

Kenneth approached the ball carrier warily. The left midfielder made a run inside. Cody cut across, and the ball carrier decided not to risk the pass. He sent it back to his defence.

"Get the ball," Luca yelled.

"Coming right up," Kenneth said over his shoulder.

"Just do it," Luca growled.

Kenneth and Luca had been sniping at each other all game.

Paulo and Jordan converged on the ball. Kenneth and William pushed up also.

"Don't go too far inside," Luca warned Cody. "They might swing it wide."

Cody moved closer to the sidelines. Trevor had talked to him about drifting out of his position. Part of the learning curve of playing midfield, Trevor had said. He must've asked Luca to help Cody, because Luca had been reminding him where to play all game. Cody appreciated it. But it was irritating all the same. He wasn't a midfielder. How was he supposed to know where to play?

The defender whipped the ball to the left, and his teammate sent a quick pass up the left sideline. A Clippers forward ran past Cody. The ball carrier took a stutter step and then reared back to pass. Cody turned and marked the forward in anticipation, and sure enough, the ball came his way. Luckily, the ball floated a bit, and the forward had to slow down to track it. Cody dove — and it was his head that made contact with the ball, sending it back to Luca. Both Cody and the Clippers forward fell to the turf. The forward's boot caught Cody below the ribs.

Cody pushed the kid away.

"Get up," Luca cried.

Luca needed an outlet. Cody ignored the pain in his ribs, and leapt to his feet. The Clippers player got up slowly.

"Use me," Cody called to Luca.

Luca flicked the ball to Cody at the last possible moment. Cody immediately took the ball inside. The Clippers forward was too slow getting up and couldn't head Cody off. Paulo was fifteen feet away. Cody passed it to him and continued up the right side. Paulo whirled with the ball on his left foot and lofted a soft chip pass over the head of the Clippers left midfielder.

Cody took the ball without breaking stride. He knew Paulo would be following up. Jordan was on the far left. Stafa was also in support. Four Clippers defenders waited.

Stafa cut toward him without warning. For a second, Cody thought he was going to take the ball off him. Instead, Stafa continued running to the sideline. Cody got it — Stafa was creating an overlap. Cody turned it on. He headed straight for the gap between the two left defenders, which forced them to shift closer together. As soon as they did, Cody faked a pass left to Paulo. Then he swung his left foot for a no-look pass to the right, where he hoped Stafa would be.

Cody's momentum sent him hurtling to the ground. He landed on his sore ribs, skidding along the grass. Some dried mud tore into his thigh. He barely felt it, absorbed by Stafa's wild charge on net. Stafa was going full-out. The goalie came out hard to meet him. They were going to collide.

"Shoot!" Cody yelled.

Stafa stuck his left foot out and lofted the ball over the startled goalie's head. Then he spun completely around the goalie, brought the ball down under control, and calmly rolled it into the gaping open net. As always, Stafa raced to the corner flag. Cody lay back down and looked up at the sky. He'd seen enough of Stafa's goal celebrations, not that the striker hadn't earned the right. That was a beautiful goal, showing huge skill. The rest of the Lions had charged to the Clippers end to celebrate. Cody wanted to enjoy the moment by himself. The game had to be almost over. A few more minutes and they'd be in the playoffs.

Paulo peered down at him. "You getting up any time soon?"

Luca joined Paulo and they both held out a hand. Cody pulled himself up.

"Anyone can break up an attack, counter it himself, and then make a perfect pass for a breakaway. So don't get too comfortable on this team. You suck, Dorsett, and I'm embarrassed to know you," Luca said.

Cody chuckled, but something was missing. Luca's joke was funny. It needed another joke to make it really funny, though. It needed Kenneth.

"Let's go congratulate Stafa," Cody said. "That was a seriously sweet goal."

Stafa had earned it. Cody knew he couldn't have scored

that goal. Even Paulo couldn't. He didn't have the foot speed.

When Kenneth saw Luca, he put his head down and jogged back to the Lions end. Luca wasn't talking to Kenneth. It seemed Kenneth had made the same decision.

21

"Come on, Cody," his mom said. "You're dragging along and we're late."

His mom waited for him in front of Stafa's house.

"We don't have to do this if you don't want," she said. "I don't care if you play Premier or stay with the Lions. We were invited to this meeting with the coaches, though — and you told me you wanted to come. It would be a bit rude if we don't show up," she said.

"I'll go. It's not that. It's . . ." It would take an hour to explain all the things going on in his head about the Lions and Kenneth and Luca. "I'm good."

Cody could hear the murmur of voices as they entered the house. Stafa's mom came out of the living room to greet them. "Hi, Cheryl. Hi, Cody. Welcome. Glad you could make it. We're about to start. I think everyone's here."

"Sorry, Rita," Cody's mom said, looking at her watch. "We're not late, I hope. I thought you said eight o'clock."

"Not at all," Rita said. "People came a bit early. They're all so excited about the team." She nodded at Cody. "That was a wonderful pass you made to Mustafa this morning. He so desperately wanted to get the team into the playoffs. It was all he and his father have been talking about for days. 'Three wins and we get the hardware,'" she giggled. "Mustafa made a poster with that phrase and taped it to the wall in his bedroom." She giggled again. "Soccer — that's all he thinks about."

It occurred to Cody that he'd been thinking about a lot of things other than soccer this season. Maybe that wasn't a bad thing.

"Come on in," Rita said. She showed them to the living room.

Stafa's house was filled with Persian-looking carpets and antiques. The place was jam-packed with furniture, candlesticks, silver-clad objects, and lamps.

Cody spotted Kenneth and David standing in front of a colourful painting. "I'll just go over there," he said to his mom. He had to pick his way around players and parents. It was standing room only.

Kenneth flicked his eyebrows. "Have you seen the play-off draw yet?" he said to Cody. He pulled out a piece of paper and gave it to him.

"South lost to AFC?" Cody exclaimed. "So we got fifth. That means we don't have to play United until the finals."

"And we play the Storm in the semis if we beat Queensland in the first round," David said pointedly.

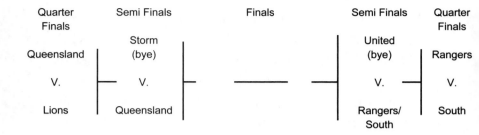

Quarter Finals	Semi Finals	Finals	Semi Finals	Quarter Finals
Queensland	Storm (bye)		United (bye)	Rangers
V.	V.		V.	V.
Lions	Queensland		Rangers/ South	South

Kenneth leaned closer. "By the way, have you noticed this room is a Timothy-free zone?"

Cody felt a smile burst out. Timothy hadn't been asked. Then the good feeling disappeared. "Antonio is here," he said.

"We don't have to be best friends with everyone on the team to play on it," Kenneth said. "Besides, without Timothy, Antonio won't be so bad. Benji and Ed won't put up with any garbage. Neither will Marco and the United boys."

Cody wasn't so sure. "Are you guys committed?" he said.

"You're not?" Kenneth said. "Didn't they offer you a spot?"

"Benji talked to my mom," Cody said. "They probably want me to play midfield and a bit of forward. It's just that . . . I like playing for the Lions. I like playing for Trevor, and with all the guys. With you guys too."

"I feel bad about that," Kenneth said, "I should've told them, especially Luca. I got too psyched about the idea — and took the secrecy thing too far."

"I went to Luca's house this weekend and told him everything," Cody said. "I think he's bummed because the Lions are breaking up."

"It's the Premier division, bro," Kenneth said, almost breathlessly. "This is big. A few guys in Premier get scholarships every year, and some have even gone pro."

Benji held his hand up and the chatter slowly died down. "Thank you all for coming out on this balmy Wednesday night," he said. "Hopefully, we get this weather for Championship Weekend."

A few kids cheered.

"We're really excited about the talent in this room," Benji continued. "Now that the regular season has ended, we can formally make offers and sign kids up for next season. We'd like to make offers to all of you guys."

The kids and parents let out a louder cheer. Cody clapped to be polite. He caught Antonio looking at him and they locked eyes for a second. Antonio looked away first.

"Right now, we want to outline our ideas for the season. After, the boys can introduce themselves to each other, although a lot of you know each other as opponents on the field of battle."

Most of the guys laughed.

"Ed is handing out an information package to the parents. It has a general schedule — practices, number of games, tournaments," Benji said. "We'll firm everything up in the spring. We are definitely going to the Schwan's Cup in Minneapolis, the largest tournament, I think, in North America. It usually has over a thousand teams. We'd also like to go to the MSC Kick-Off Classic in New York. And maybe the Dallas Cup, one of the oldest tourneys around. It's critical we gain experience against a wide variety of teams and styles. We want to keep this team together for a few years. We really believe this group can be special."

"I've put together a schedule for the off-season," Ed said. "We'll practise three times a week, have some indoor tournaments, and play a limited twenty-game season. I'll go over our training targets and nutritional goals later."

"At least they're not taking it seriously," Cody joked to Kenneth.

Kenneth didn't laugh.

"Awesome," Benji said. "Please let me have your attention here on the screen. Ed, can you turn on the projector?"

A chart appeared.

The parents all watched closely as Benji described the tournaments and explained how scholarships were awarded. Most of the guys listened closely too. Cody saw Stafa whisper to his dad. Gary shook his head. Stafa folded his arms across his chest. Then he reached behind his dad's back to grab a big chocolate cupcake from the dessert table. He took a bite before his father snatched the cupcake from him.

"It's a lot of soccer," Cody whispered to David.

David grinned and flashed a thumbs-up.

Cody took a deep breath. No choice but to listen. Benji continued on for another twenty minutes. Then Ed did a presentation on fitness and nutrition. They finally finished, and people began to mingle. Cody tried to get his mom's attention, but she was talking to some other parents.

"Good luck this weekend." Marco offered a friendly grin and swept his long hair from his face.

"We're not exactly upset to miss you guys in the semis," Kenneth said.

"We have the Lions pegged to get through," Marco said. He glanced over his shoulder. "Please don't let the Storm make it."

"It'll break my heart to see Timothy all teary-eyed when they lose," Kenneth said.

"Maybe he'll see it as an opportunity for growth," David said.

"Fat chance." Kenneth snickered.

"You guys hear about Timothy's dad?" Marco said. "Ian offered to sponsor this team — pay for everything — even fly us to England to train with Manchester United's youth development squad. Only condition was Timothy had to be the striker."

"I guess we're not going to Europe," Kenneth said.

Marco chuckled. "I think we have other sponsorships lined up. Benji's dad is supposedly loaded."

"Lots of pressure on us to win," Cody said.

"It's Premier," Marco said. "Every game will be a war."

Cody's mom waved to him by the hallway where she was talking to Ed.

"I gotta go," Cody said. "Good luck to you, Marco. See you in the finals, I hope."

"No hope. It'll happen." Marco grinned.

"You psyched for this?" Ed asked Cody as he approached.

"A lot of soccer, anyway," Cody said.

Ed nodded. "That it will be. We're excited to have you with us. We love your versatility, up front with Stafa or in the midfield. We obviously haven't settled on positions and formations yet. We need to watch more video, too."

Video?

"It sounds like you have things well organized, Ed," Cody's mom said.

"We do," Ed said, with a big smile. "We'll get the paperwork going in a minute. Why don't you guys get something to eat?"

"Do you want to sign the commitment now or think about it a bit?" his mom said to Cody.

"I guess I'll think about it," Cody said.

The smile faded from Ed's face.

"We should get going," his mom said. "Cody, can you say thank you to Gary and Rita for hosting?"

Cody went back into the room. Fortunately, Rita noticed him.

"Do you have to go, Cody?" Rita said.

Stafa's mom seemed nice. He liked her.

"Be sharp on Saturday," Gary snapped. "Stafa needs more ball inside the box if we're going to win."

And then there was his dad.

"Oh, stop for once." Rita laughed. "The boys will do their best. Thanks for coming, Cody."

"Thanks for having me and my mom," Cody said.

Gary grunted and turned back to Benji. "I don't like that MSC Kick-Off Classic. It's too local."

Cody and his mom left.

For a while in the car, he and his mom listened to the radio. Then she lowered the volume. *Here it comes*, thought Cody.

"Well, Cody, is this a team you want to play for?"

"Doesn't it depend on where we're living?"

"I suppose. But let's assume we stay. What then?"

"Not sure."

"You need to make a decision. They want a commitment."

"How about maybe?"

She smiled. "What does your gut tell you?"

"That I should've had one of those cupcakes?"

She laughed and turned the radio back up. Cody was grateful that they didn't have to talk. He honestly didn't know what to do. It was like he was being pulled in two directions with equal force. The idea of playing Premier was cool. He'd be lying to himself if he didn't admit that. He wondered what would it be like to play with the best players, really test himself. What was stopping him? Was he afraid of the competition? Was it nerves? Was he doubting himself? Mandy and Talia played in the top girls' league and they never complained.

His time would be taken up by practices, games, tournaments, training. He loved soccer — but did he love it as much as Stafa obviously did?

Then there were the Lions. If Cody, Kenneth, David, Stafa, and Paulo left, was there a team? They'd only have seven players. They could recruit, but it would be a different group of guys.

Cody stared out the window. Before he got sick, life was about having fun. During the cancer treatments, he told himself that when he got better he'd have fun all the time and never worry about anything. That was not the way it had turned out.

Cody didn't know where to start. Maybe he should talk to someone and get another opinion. Kenneth? Then Luca might be mad. Luca? Same with Kenneth. Both of them at once? They weren't talking to each other. Paulo? He was leaving in four days. So who?

22

Cody's fingers hovered over the keyboard. He'd spent the rest of the day and most of the night after the Premier team meeting trying to make a decision. Here it was, a day later, three o'clock in the afternoon, and he still didn't have a clue what he should do.

For the last hour he'd been on Facebook with Mandy. Somehow their messages had gotten serious. He read her last one.

It's like what you said, that being sick, with something like cancer, is almost easier than watching someone in your family go through it. I can't find the right words, only I think about Gavin and all the time we spent in the hospital, and then about the times we thought he was getting better, and then when he wasn't. I

139

never really thought he wouldn't get better, not really. It's like I wouldn't accept what was happening right in front of my eyes. Gavin was like this perfect kid, and he had to go through this terrible thing. I'm, like . . . definitely not this perfect kid, and I was totally healthy. I felt guilty all the time, like I should be the one with cancer, not him. Does that even make sense? Nothing makes sense right now. Sorry for all this. I'm rambling and being depressing.

Cody wrote back.

I think it's normal, feeling guilty I mean. I used to feel bad about how my cancer made my mom and dad so upset, and also how it made other people feel uncomfortable. I felt like I should apologize. Sounds dumb, but that's the way it was, even now a bit. Obviously, it wasn't my fault I got sick or lost my hair. I felt guilty about it, anyway. So I can see why you'd feel bad being healthy when Gavin was so sick. I bet you felt like you were showing off — running around the soccer field when your brother could barely get the energy to walk. But like me, it's not your fault. You shouldn't feel guilty.

Her message came back almost immediately.

That's what drives me mad. I know I shouldn't feel guilty about being healthy. Then I act so mean to people because I'm upset, even though I know I'm being mean only because I feel guilty. I can't stop myself, somehow. I need to wash my brain!!!

He tried to think of something funny. He didn't feel like being funny, though.

You're always hard on yourself, even when we play soccer. Every mistake makes you mad. I've seen you. You smack your thigh and say, 'Stupid Mandy,' sometimes even when it's not a mistake, like when maybe you just tried something in a pickup game and it didn't work, and sometimes when it's the other player's fault. It's like you want to blame yourself for everything. Does that make sense?

Again, Mandy responded right away.

That's it, exactly — like it makes me feel better to feel bad. Fix me!

He typed a message quickly, without thinking.

You don't need to be fixed. You are fine.

She didn't answer for a couple of minutes.
He wrote,

Are you still there?

Another minute went by.

Yup. Just thinking. Any ideas of how to feel better?

Cody considered her question for a while, and then wrote,

I think I started to feel less guilty when I stopped thinking about me all the time. First, it was being a good teammate. Then it was helping you guys fight against the factory at Lake Tawson. Then maybe trying to be a good friend to you. And don't tell anyone, but now it's about trying to get Kenneth and Luca to be friends again. Not sure about those two. I still have to decide about next season myself. I feel like I'm betraying the Lions if I leave.

Cody stopped and read over what he'd written: *good friend to you . . . decide about next season*. Here he was telling Mandy that he had this difficult decision to make, and he didn't know what to do with Kenneth and Luca. He hadn't asked for her opinion. Why not? She and Talia had a serious fight and they got through it. And she'd been playing Premier soccer for a few years. She'd know way better than him what Premier was like. He deleted the message and wrote,

Kinda bored. You wanna get an ice cream?

Cody looked at his message. He took a deep breath and then hit the Return key to send it. A sweat broke out at the back of his neck. He was so uncool. He stared at the screen. No answer. She was probably trying to figure out how to get out of it.

A message popped up.

Sure. See you there in 20 minutes.

He read it again, almost not believing. He then heard footsteps. He logged out of his Facebook account.

"Cody, I need my laptop. It's called work," his mom said.

"Sorry. Just had to check something."

"I'm sure it was incredibly important. Now scoot. And find something to do, preferably that doesn't involve technology."

He got up from the table. "So, Mom, is it okay for me to meet someone? Get an ice cream or something?"

"Sure. Who are you meeting?"

"Just soccer friends."

"No problem. We might need to eat dinner a bit early, so make sure you're back by six."

"Okay, Mom. I'll be back way before that." He cleared his throat. "Um . . . could I maybe have a little money?"

She laughed and reached into her purse on the counter. "Here's twenty dollars. A little change will be appreciated — and expected."

"It won't be that much. Thanks. See you for dinner."

He grabbed his bike from the garage and set off. His nerves kicked in for some reason. He kept telling himself it was no big deal. Didn't help. It felt like a big deal. He was being so dumb. He pedalled harder. He didn't want to be late.

By the time Cody arrived at the ice cream shop he felt more excited than nervous. He locked his bike and peered in through the window. Mandy was sitting along the wall at a table. Without warning, his stomach felt unsettled.

He gripped the door handle and hesitated. Four people were waiting for him to go in, so he had no choice. He pushed the door open. Mandy waved from across the room and smiled. He forced himself to smile back.

"How's it going?" he said, sitting across from her.

"Okay, I guess."

"Big weekend — championships and all. I'm a bit nervous. Your team will crush it, I'm sure."

"I hope."

A server came over. "You decided yet?"

"You want to share a banana split?" Mandy said.

"Sure," Cody said.

"You get three flavours," the server said.

"What do you want?" Mandy asked him.

He suddenly couldn't think of a flavour other than chocolate or vanilla.

"I'm fine — whatever you want," he managed.

"Oookay," Mandy said. "How about mocha almond fudge, cookies and cream, and burnt caramel?"

"Sounds good," Cody said.

He hated those flavours.

"Shouldn't take too long," the server said. She went to another table.

Mandy twisted her hand. Her two gold bracelets fell down her arm.

"I noticed those on the beach," Cody said. "They're nice. Where'd you get them?"

She looked up at him. "They're my mom's. I just feel like wearing them. Makes me feel like we're close — even when we're not living together."

"How's your mom doing?"

She flushed. "I've gone every day since you took me. I was there this morning for a couple hours. We talk and hang out or watch TV. I've learned a lot about how she feels. I think I was a bit harsh. I was so upset I blamed her, like it was her fault she has depression. And then I felt guilty about not being sick and . . . A nurse talked to me about it. She said it's very common for healthy family members to feel bad about being healthy. She told me that the best thing is to talk about it. Me and mom have tried — maybe we could do more. It's hard to talk about stuff like that to your mom. Parents aren't supposed to have problems." She laughed, but not in a happy way. "Anyway, I've learned that she's had depression since she was young. So . . . obviously it's not my fault. When Gavin died it triggered these black feelings, like she couldn't get happy again . . ." She lowered her eyes.

Cody gave her hand a gentle squeeze. "It's been hard for you too."

"I feel bad about how I've been acting," she said. "I went into my own world and got mad at mom for being sad. Real nice. She needed me, probably more than I needed her."

"I did the same thing," Cody said. "My mom worries about me so much, and I get mad at her for worrying. I think I want things to be normal so bad that I get angry when she reminds me about having cancer. It's like it's okay when I mention it, but I hate when anyone else does."

Mandy wiped her eyes with a napkin. "Mom says my visits do more for her than all the medication and the doctors combined. I think she says that to make me visit. Doesn't matter. I like going . . . So I sit with her and . . . we just sit together . . ." Her voice trailed off.

"Do you think she's feeling better?"

A smile flickered. "She says she's feeling a hundred times better. But it's only been three visits, and that's my mom for you. Always over the top. I think that she's trying to feel better, and that's important. The doctors think she can go home soon. She also wants to go back to work. She likes working."

"It's good to have a goal, I bet."

Mandy took a deep breath. "I think it is."

"One banana split," the server said. She put the dish between them. "I assume two spoons are in order."

Mandy frowned. "Um . . . not really. This is for me." She pulled the dish toward her.

Cody felt himself turn red. "I'm okay. I ate before I came."

Mandy burst out laughing and pushed the plate back to the middle. "Two spoons works. Thanks," she said.

"You're a bad girl," Cody said as the server walked away. "That definitely earned you a time out."

Mandy scooped some ice cream and popped it into her mouth. "Dig in, or you won't get any. I could seriously eat the whole thing."

Cody took a bite.

"So, what's the Cody report?"

He felt silly talking about the Premier team, but he needed to talk to someone — a friend. And he had the feeling she would want him to talk to her. "I guess I'm a little bummed about the championship this weekend. Kenneth and David are leaving the team, so the Lions will never be the same. And then there's the fact that Kenneth and Luca aren't talking to each other."

"Talia told me about those two. What's the deal?"

Cody filled her in quickly.

"Not like I have the right to judge peoples' behaviour," said Mandy. "But it seems to me that when you do something wrong you should apologize for it. And if you're sincere, the other person usually forgives you. At least, that's what happened with me."

Cody thought about his conversation with Luca. Kenneth had to admit his mistakes too.

Mandy eyed him carefully. "Is Cody Dorsett signing with a Premier team?"

He looked up to the ceiling. "Cody Dorsett is being a wuss and can't make up his mind. On top of everything, my parents are thinking of moving back to Ferguson."

Mandy's face fell.

"We probably won't go," he added hurriedly. "Like almost for sure we won't, but it's an idea."

She poked her spoon into the ice cream. "I hope you stay," she said simply.

"So do I."

Did he mean it? He wasn't sure. He knew it would be sad to live so far away from Mandy.

Mandy pressed her lips together. "Why don't you want to play Premier?"

"I sorta do. It would be a huge step up. The other guys are real good. Maybe I'm nervous about that. What do you think I should do?"

"You're obviously good enough or they wouldn't have picked you."

"Stafa's the striker. I think they'll want me to play midfield." He put his spoon down. "You know, it hit me last game. Stafa's a better striker than me — and he's a year younger. That guy's unreal. Do I want to be a midfielder and maybe not even make the starting eleven? Or do I stay on the Lions and be the striker? I like playing with the Lions, with Trevor. I feel disloyal, like I'm quitting on them."

"Do you know any guys on the Premier team, other than Kenneth and David?"

"A little — we had a practice and a team meeting. They seem okay. Except for one guy, Antonio, who plays for the Storm. We don't exactly get along. By that I mean we hate each other. At least they didn't ask Timothy. Then I definitely wouldn't have played for them."

"It's just one guy, then?"

"Yeah. Then there's the fact that it's completely over-the-top. We're going all over the place for tournaments and there are so many practices and so much training. It's like playing pro — without the money."

Mandy dipped her spoon into a pool of melted ice cream. "This is the best part. You get the ice cream mixed with the chocolate sauce."

"Stop hogging it all, then," Cody said. He reached his spoon out.

She blocked his spoon with hers.

"Sounds like Cody needs to decide who he is," she said.

"What do you mean?"

"Are you someone who wants to push himself and maybe fail? Or would you rather just play for fun and not worry about trying to win all the time?" she said. "I don't know what's best for you. I've seen kids forced to play by their parents so they'll get university scholarships. I've also seen kids who have tons of talent but they don't want to put in the work. Some kids aren't that into soccer. Some kids don't have the confidence." She moved her spoon away. "So who are you, Cody?

Her words felt like a heavy weight on his shoulders, because he couldn't answer the question.

She ducked her head and leaned forward. "So . . ."

"Can I think about it?" He laughed.

She scooped some of the melted ice cream. He did the same.

"On one condition. That you ask me for ice cream again — soon. It cheers me up."

"Okay — but next time I pick the flavours. I mean, mocha almond fudge? Come on. That's almost as bad as mint chocolate chip."

"I love mint," she said.

"Yuck. It's a colour, not a flavour."

"I might have to rethink this ice cream thing. I didn't know you were so pathetic at ordering."

"I'm pathetic at everything." He laughed.

"No you're not," she said, seriously.

They both got quiet and dug into the banana split.

Cody held the ice cream shop's door open for Mandy.

"I'm gonna have to fake dinner," he said, holding his stomach. "We're eating early and I'm stuffed."

"Their banana split is hefty," Mandy said as they walked along the sidewalk.

"You shouldn't have paid for it," he said.

"You can get the next one."

"Okay, that's fair."

"When's your first game tomorrow?"

"Ten o'clock. I'm coming to watch you and Talia play at eight thirty."

"We better play well," she said.

They turned the corner.

"Oh, look! It's Egg-Head and his pet chimp."

Timothy stood ten feet away, laughing, Michael and

Tyler on one side and Antonio on the other. John peered over Antonio's shoulder, a few feet back. Cody reached out and held Mandy's arm to stop.

"Use a leash, it's easier," Timothy said.

"Shut up," Mandy snapped.

"Does your dog bite?" Tyler said.

Five against one — not good odds. He couldn't get Mandy involved in this. He also couldn't look like a wuss in front of her. Cody knew Timothy was a bully — and bullies always back down.

"Be a loser on your own time," Cody said. "We're busy."

"Woooo," Timothy, Tyler, and Michael mocked.

"I ain't got time for your garbage," Cody said.

"Really. You actually think you're a tough guy?" Timothy said. He took a few steps toward Cody.

Cody's heart was racing. *Show no fear*, he told himself. He stepped forward.

"Look at the brave man. Don't worry. I won't hurt your pet, just you," Timothy said to Cody.

"Takes a tough guy to make threats when you have me outnumbered five to one," Cody said. He prayed his voice didn't sound scared.

"Let's go, Timothy," Antonio said. "We don't need this."

"'Cause he's gonna be your teammate?" Timothy sneered.

Antonio's face hardened. "Yeah, maybe. This is dumb. Let's forget it and go."

"It'll be the biggest mistake of your life if you play with Humpty Dumpty," Timothy said. "And that loser Kenneth. Go for it, bro. My dad is talking to five Premier teams.

152

Only question is who I sign with. Tyler and Michael too. You really want to play with Humpty Dumpty instead of us?"

Antonio shifted uneasily from foot to foot. "It's just a soccer team, bro. Lighten up."

Cody was surprised. Antonio seemed like a different kid. He wasn't acting tough, as usual. Was Timothy right? Was Antonio acting like this because he thought he and Cody would be teammates on the Premier team? Some guys were jerks to everyone but their teammates. Antonio had given Cody a hard time when they were on the Lions. But Cody was the new kid — and he'd been bald, a bit of a target. One thing was clear. Antonio didn't want to fight now.

"You're right. My bad. I should lighten up. I don't know why I get so crazed about stuff. It's just soccer," Timothy said.

Cody relaxed. His hunch had paid off. Timothy had backed down, like always. He felt a surge of pride as he turned to Mandy. "Let's —"

Timothy's fist hit Cody square in the cheek. Cody fell to the ground, stunned by the blow.

"Get up, tough guy. C'mon Egg-Head," Timothy roared. He was standing over Cody.

Cody rolled up onto his knees. Timothy threw a left hook into his ribs. Cody felt the wind go out of him. But his rage gave him the strength to throw his shoulder into Timothy's legs and knock him down. Timothy kicked his left foot out and caught Cody in the chest. Cody was beyond caring about the pain. He drove and ploughed

153

Timothy in the side of the head with a right hook of his own. Timothy wrapped his arms around Cody's shoulders.

Then Cody felt Timothy slipping away.

"What's wrong with you?" Timothy raged.

Antonio had pulled him off Cody.

"He's a dead man. Completely dead!" Timothy yelled.

John helped Cody to his feet.

"Timothy, this is . . . We gotta play tomorrow. Not worth it," Antonio said. He held Timothy's shirt with both hands.

Timothy pushed him away. "It is worth it," Timothy said. "Totally worth it. But whatever. That's just a taste, Egg Whites. This ain't over."

"You're pathetic, Timothy, but at least you're consistent," Cody said.

Kenneth and Luca would've loved that one.

"Next time, I hit you for real," Timothy said, with a cocky grin.

"For real, as in when I'm not looking?" Cody said.

"Keep your guard up, Humpty," Timothy said. He laughed meanly and marched down the street.

Tyler and Michael followed Timothy. They looked back a few times, but kept going. Antonio and John didn't move.

"You okay?" Antonio asked Cody.

Cody wiped his face with his hand. "Bit of a nosebleed, I think." He pressed his nose to stop the blood. His ribs and chest hurt too. But he wasn't going to admit it. "I'm fine." He didn't want Mandy to think he couldn't take it.

"That guy is unbelievable," Mandy fumed.

"That's his style," Cody said. "I should've been ready."

Antonio looked down the street at Timothy's back, then

turned back to Cody. "I know you and I are going to be playing together next season. Benji talked to me about . . . being a good teammate and stuff. Anyway, I know I've said some stupid things. I've been a jerk. It's just that . . . Timothy makes me act like an idiot." He blew air between his lips. "You sure you're okay?"

"Yeah. He doesn't hit that hard," Cody said.

Not exactly true, but he figured Mandy would be impressed.

"See you tomorrow, Cody," Antonio said. "You win your first game against Queensland and we play you in the semis."

"Good luck," Cody said.

Antonio held out his hand. Cody hesitated and then took it. This was beyond weird. All of a sudden Antonio is a nice guy because Cody was going to be on his soccer team?

Weirdest part was that Cody understood.

Antonio nodded at John. "You coming?"

"Go ahead," John said. "I'm done with Timothy."

"Me too. I'm going home," Antonio said. He headed up the street, leaving the three of them behind.

Cody looked at John. He'd been just as brutal to Cody as Timothy at the start of the season. Now he looked like a sad, scared little kid.

John nodded toward Antonio, about fifty feet away by then. "Antonio isn't a bad guy," he said to Cody. "He was okay until Timothy and Ian changed him. He became this tough guy. I've known him for years, since grade three . . ." John sighed. "I know it's easy to blame Timothy for

155

everything. He has this way of getting you to do what he says. You want him to like you, and you don't want him to turn on you. So you act tough. You bully and yell at guys. But it's not all Timothy's fault. We should make up our own minds. I think we fell for Ian's promises. He said we were going to Europe to train and we were going to be an awesome Premier team and have the best coaches. We all fell for it, players and parents. But now everyone knows Timothy's bailing on the Storm. He'll play Premier for someone, and Ian will pay for it."

At least he's not playing for Benji, Cody thought.

"Good luck with Championship Weekend. I probably won't touch the field. They never play me," John said. "I don't really care. I'm finished with the Storm. My dad's done too. Ian doesn't know it yet, but my dad's going to quit working for him. We're going to move to the west coast. My dad's going to be the accountant for my uncle's construction business."

"That's . . . a big change," Cody said.

"Tough to leave all your friends and go so far away," Mandy said.

John gave her an odd smile. "Not as hard as you'd think," he said.

"Thanks — for breaking the fight up," Cody said.

"Timothy took a cheap shot," John said. "And trust me, I'll make sure everyone knows that." He looked closely at Cody's face. "I think you might have a black eye."

Cody touched his cheek. His mom would freak, and he'd have a lot of questions to answer from teammates.

John pointed up the hill. "I guess I'll get going. I pick

you and United in the finals."

John held out his hand. Cody shook it gladly. John smiled, but he looked sad all the same. Then he left, walking slowly, barely picking his heels up, as if deep in thought.

"If he moves away, he can get a fresh start, be the kid he wants to be. No one knows him there. This will be a good thing for him," Cody said.

"Moving wouldn't be a good thing for you. You belong here," Mandy said.

Cody hung his head. "Can't believe Timothy knocked me down. I'm so bogus."

"You are not," she said hotly. "You weren't ready. Even John and Antonio said it was a cheap shot. Besides, who cares? Boys . . . fighting. It's dumb. There are more important things in life than the Championship Weekend."

Cody reached out and pulled her in for a hug. He figured she needed one — and maybe he did too?

"You tell your mom you're staying," she whispered in his ear. "Tell her I won't let you go."

"I'll tell her," Cody said. "And I should get back. My mom said —"

"I know, an early dinner."

He laughed. "See you. Good luck tomorrow. I'll be watching."

"I'll watch you too. Be strong on the ball!"

He laughed and headed up the hill.

"Hey, Cody."

He turned.

"What do you want me to do with your bike?"

He let his shoulders slump.

"Hit me over the head with it. I'm too stupid to have one."

She grinned. "I'll ride back with you partway — in case Timothy tries something."

"I'll keep my hands up this time."

"No doubt."

She slipped her arm through his and together they walked back to the ice cream store for his bike.

25

The girls were almost finished their warm-ups. Talia was kicking on goal with a few other forwards. Mandy was playing keep-away with the rest of the team. To Cody, she looked slight and wispy in her uniform, as if she'd break in two if someone so much as touched her. He knew better. On the field she was practically unstoppable, fearless, and had more skills than anyone he knew other than maybe Paulo — or Stafa.

Mandy had the ball. She spun around a girl, ball dragging in her right foot. Then she adroitly skipped a pass between another girl's legs.

"Hi, Cody," a soft voice from behind him said.

It was Mandy's mom. "Hi, Candice. How are you?" he said, surprised to see her.

"I'm feeling much better," she smiled. "Nice to be

outside, anyway. Are you playing today?"

"We play later. I wanted to watch Mandy's game a bit. They'll win, for sure. They came first in the league."

"So you said," she chuckled. "Um . . . you hurt yourself?" she said, pointing to his eye.

John had been right. Cody had woken up with a shiner. He touched it.

"It's nothing. Banged myself — a door."

"It looks painful. Are you sure you can play?"

"For sure. It's no big deal."

Her eyes became fixed and her smile grew faint. "I wanted to thank you for bringing Mandy to the hospital. It was very kind of you. And I especially want to thank you for finding her at the lake. She told me what happened."

"She was upset and wanted to get away," Cody said. "She'd have come back. And the hospital was her idea. I just came along . . ."

Candice touched his shoulder. "I know this is awkward. I've embarrassed her, and you're uncomfortable talking about it. That's okay."

"I think she understands," he said quickly. "And I'm not uncomfortable about it. I was sick too, and spent a lot of time in that hospital. So I sort of get it more than most people." He looked over to the field. They were doing the coin flip. "I'm glad you're feeling better, Candice."

She ran a hand over her hair. "It's wonderful to hear your cancer treatment was successful." Her eyes clouded.

"I'm real sorry about Gavin," Cody said.

Candice wiped away a tear. "That's sweet of you to say. It's funny, but I like to hear his name."

"Mandy said he was a pretty cool kid. That I would've liked him."

"Everyone liked my Gavin. He was . . ." Candice gave her head a shake. "All moms love their kids. Mandy's wonderful too. I've let her down, and that's made it harder to get over . . . this." Suddenly, she laughed and gave his shoulder a squeeze. "Let's not go there. You have a game to play. And I'm darn tired of being sad. I've promised my doctor that I would be happy today, and I don't want to break my promise."

"That's a good promise to keep," Cody said.

He used to do the same thing when he'd been going through his cancer treatments. He'd ignore the pain and watch funny movies and TV shows and laugh his head off. His parents and the nurses thought he was crazy. And maybe he was, but it helped.

"Well . . . I see Sharon over there. I'll go say hi. Nice to see you, Cody."

"Same . . . Bye."

When Candice reached Talia's mom, Sharon threw her arms around her neck. The two women hugged for a long time.

"It's Championship Weekend, ladies and gentlemen," Kenneth said, in a pretend announcer's voice. He came over. "Hold on to your hats. It's going to be *in-sane!*"

Cody and Kenneth slapped hands.

"Too psyched to sleep in," Kenneth said. "My parents dropped me off and went for breakfast." He looked down the sidelines. "Mandy's mom? Is she . . . okay?"

"Yeah, but I think she needs more time," Cody said.

"Tough on Mandy. Good to hear things are better."
Kenneth stopped short. "What happened to you?" he said,
pointing to Cody's eye.

"Timmer and I had a discussion yesterday. Apparently,
he disagreed with me about what colour goes best with
grey pants."

Kenneth's eyes opened wide. "Grey is neutral. You can
wear what you want."

"That's what I said." Cody laughed.

"Seriously, bro. What happened?" Kenneth said.

"I ran into Timothy and his crew after getting some ice
cream. One thing lead to another and then . . . *POW!*" He
punched a fist into his palm.

"Timothy's amazing. Just when you think he can't be a
bigger jerk, he is."

Cody noticed Leandro's car pull into the lot. "Before
the guys show, I thought . . . Hey, it's not me telling you
what to do. But I went to Luca's house and apologized for
lying about the Premier team when he asked me about it.
Maybe . . . you should do the same?"

"Why can't I play Premier?" Kenneth said hotly. "Everyone acts like I don't care about the Lions. I've been to all
the games and practices —"

"Guys want you to be honest," Cody said.

"I told them last practice. And I apologized," Kenneth
said.

"I know, but maybe Luca expects something more . . .
personal?"

Kenneth didn't react so quickly this time. "I'll think
about it," he said finally.

"Cool." Cody didn't want to push it. It was Kenneth's decision.

"Have you made up your mind — about Premier?" Kenneth asked.

"Yo, boys. What up?" Paulo called out before Cody could answer.

"Paulo, check Cody out. Timothy and he dropped the gloves and went at it," Kenneth said.

"Get out. When?"

"Yesterday afternoon," Cody said. "I was . . . getting some ice cream."

"With who?" Paulo said.

Why did he ask that? "Um . . . I, um, met Mandy there." Kenneth and Paulo looked at each other.

"We're not going to just ignore that, are we?" Kenneth said. They both burst out laughing.

"How was the date?" Paulo said, finally.

"It wasn't a date," Cody said. "We met for —"

"A girl and a boy meeting for ice cream is a date," Kenneth declared. "I read it on the Internet somewhere . . . Maybe a *dating* website?"

"So if you and Talia met for ice cream, would that be a date?" Cody said. He knew for a fact they'd done that a few times.

"No. We're friends." Kenneth grinned.

"So are Mandy and me," Cody said.

"A date," Kenneth and Paulo said, in unison.

"Gentlemen, how are the ladies doing?"

It was Luca. The smile left Luca's face when he saw Kenneth.

163

"Cody was on a date with Mandy yesterday, and he got into a fight with Timothy," Paulo said.

"I don't know which piece of info is more interesting. Let's start with the fight," Luca said.

"The idiot hit me when I wasn't looking," Cody said. "He pretended to leave and then smoked me one. Weird part is that Antonio pulled Timothy off me and apologized to me for acting like a jerk. He kinda blamed it on Timothy. Not sure what to think about that. But he obviously wants things to be good on the Premier team — if I play, I mean."

The whistle went. The girls' game had begun. Cody gathered his nerve. The feud between Kenneth and Luca had to end.

26

This might get messy, but this was what friends did.

Cody started, "Guys, we all know the situation. We all know that nothing can stay the same. Not a soccer team, not school, not friends, not even your family."

His teammates were listening intently.

"Do we need to ruin everything because things are going to change?" he continued. "It's not like we were going to play for the Lions until we were eighty. I don't care about what team I play for next season, or what team Kenneth or Luca plays for, as much as I care about the Lions this season, right now." He glared at Kenneth and Luca. "Are we gonna stop hanging out at Lake Tawson and playing pickup at the park because of a dumb soccer team?"

The two boys looked at each other for a few moments.

"I didn't really know how to tell you this, Cody . . ." Kenneth's voice got quiet.

Luca cleared his throat. "I'll just come out and say it. Of course, we're gonna hang at the lake and play pickup," Luca said. "It's just that . . ." He turned his head and pressed his lips together. He couldn't go on.

Kenneth patted Luca's back. "I'll do it. The thing is, Cody . . . you're not really invited," Kenneth said, a smile starting to appear.

"Sorry, but you're not awesome enough," Luca said, trying to look sad. "Not your fault."

"Totally not your fault," Kenneth said. "You just — basically — suck at everything."

Cody decided to go for it. "That's fine, because I found a bunch of awesome new friends . . . Totally awesome guys. So I wouldn't have time for you guys anyway."

"Cody . . . I'm pretty sure we're the only friends you have," Kenneth said. "And we're not even really your friends."

"Kenneth makes a fairly good point," Luca said.

"Don't want to pick sides, but I have to admit Kenneth and Luca are right," Paulo joined in.

"You guys are not cool enough to be friends with my new friends," Cody said, crossing his arms. "Trust me, they're ridiculously awesome."

"Name them," Kenneth said.

"They all have different names," Cody said. "Makes it hard to remember. So I gave them numbers. There's Friend One and Friend Two and . . . Friend Eighty-Seven. It's like a pattern, a number pattern. It's too complicated for you to understand."

"Cody's reached the imaginary friend stage," Kenneth whispered loudly to Luca. "Let it go. Little kids do it all the time."

"You have an imaginary friend," Luca said to Kenneth.

"Sebastian is different," Kenneth said. "Besides, you've met him"

Luca winked at Cody. "Yeah . . . for sure, Kenneth. I met Sebastian. And you're right, a giant talking squid is . . . different. "

Cody felt a ton of stress fall away. "Are you guys going to stop acting like idiots now?"

"I'll stop acting like an idiot because that's easy for me," Kenneth said. "But Luca can't."

"I can about the Premier team. But I'll keep being an idiot about everything else," Luca said.

Kenneth held his hand down low and Luca gave it a slap.

Luca nodded at Kenneth. "You can cry if you want. I won't think you're a huge baby even though that's what huge babies do."

"I'm about to cry because I feel sorry for you having to go through life being you," Kenneth said.

"That's sorta what a huge baby would say. So you should cry about that," Luca said.

"I don't know why, but I'm going to miss you guys," Paulo said when he stopped laughing enough to talk.

"Geez, I thought you went home already," Cody said. "Didn't notice you there."

Paulo's eyes got wide. "Not sure what's happened. Have you guys noticed that Cody actually makes jokes? And he's been doing it more and more lately."

"It's not like he's got a sense of humour or anything," Kenneth said. "But I'd say he's definitely funnier than a zombie apocalypse."

"For sure," Paulo said.

"I'd say he's even funnier than global warming and toe fungus," Luca said.

Paulo patted Cody on the back. "Wow. You've come a long way since I met you."

Kenneth took a deep breath. "Not that I want to see Luca cry, although I sorta do, but I admit I was a jerk about the Premier team. I got all into the idea of the tournaments and scholarships and . . . I'm sorry, bud." He and Luca slapped hands again.

"I would never admit to being selfish," Kenneth continued, "but I guess it goes without saying. Benji and Ed kept telling me to make the move and that it would be great. And I forgot that we're Lions — always. No matter what team we play on or where we live."

Cody figured he should come totally clean to his friends. "Just to make the point that nothing stays the same," he said, "my parents are thinking about moving back to Ferguson. I don't know what I'm going to do."

"What? You're not leaving," Kenneth said. "I won't give my permission. I made an exception for Paulo — and I still regret it."

"Case closed," Luca said. "Cody stays. And Paulo is coming back after his one-week holiday."

"Since when did we agree to an entire week?" Kenneth said.

"I'm kidding. It's only a weekend pass," Luca said.

"I get ya," Paulo said. "I've been on the Lions for only two months. But it feels like we've been playing together on the same team since we were little kids."

"That's because Kenneth is a huge baby," Luca said.

"No, that's because of the waterproof diapers I wear," Kenneth said.

"Are you sure it's not your soother?" Luca said.

"I haven't used a soother in three years," Kenneth said.

"Kenneth?"

"Fine. Eighteen months, but still."

It had been too long since Cody had listened to their nonsense. It made him realize how much he missed it. He would miss it regardless of which team he picked.

Paulo elbowed him. "So which team, bro? I bet Benji won't let you wait much longer."

Cody threw his hands in the air. "I don't know. Kenneth, I want to play with you and David. And there are guys on the team that seem cool. And like I said, even Antonio seems to have changed. Premier will be intense — a challenge. I'm not sure I want to play that much soccer, though, and go to all those tournaments. Or that I'm interested in scholarships. I like Trevor and the Lions . . . Am I sounding like a wuss?"

"You always do," Kenneth said.

"But it works for you," Luca said.

"I think I liked it better when you guys weren't talking to each other," Cody said.

"He might even be funnier than malaria," Luca said to Kenneth.

"That's a bit much," Kenneth said.

"I'm trying to encourage him," Luca said.

Cody knew better than to try to keep up with these two. So he was honest. "I love the game. I don't know if I love it more than anything else. I don't know if I'm worried about going to a new school and I don't want to deal with switching teams on top of that. I might regret it later, or it'll be the best decision I ever made. Mandy thinks I should go for it."

"Did you talk about it on your date?" Kenneth said.

Cody was about to argue — then it hit him. It *was* a date.

"We did," he said simply.

"She's a pretty intense player," Luca said.

"I don't think you're a wuss for thinking about whether you want to spend that much time playing soccer," Paulo said. "From what I've heard, Premier players are on the pitch six times a week, every weekend, twelve months a year. Kenneth and Dave are into it. You don't have to be."

Cody was surprised to hear Paulo say that. "Would you play if you were staying?" Cody said.

Paulo flashed that grin. "I'm a freak. I would. But you gotta decide for yourself what you want to do."

So Mandy, and now Paulo, were telling Cody the same thing. He had to decide what he wanted. And he couldn't do that without understanding what made Cody Dorsett tick.

"When I first got sick all I thought about was playing soccer again. Now I'm playing and I don't know," Cody said.

"It's not like your career's over if you play for the Lions,"

Luca said. "We'll have to recruit some new guys, and we might not be as good. But we'll still have a team."

"Take another year before moving up if you want," Paulo said.

"But, just so you know, you're not moving to Ferguson," Kenneth said.

The crowd next to them let out a cheer. Mandy had made a beautiful stretch pass to send Talia in alone on goal.

"Go for it, Talia!" Kenneth yelled.

Talia took a step sideways to the right, then rifled the ball across the net to the far post. The goalie looked up to the sky. A goal.

"We should get those two to play for the Lions," Luca said.

"Cody can ask Mandy . . . on their next date," Paulo said.

The boys laughed and this time Cody joined in.

"Fine, it was a date," Cody said. "Can we change the topic?"

Talia flashed a thumbs-up to them as she jogged back to centre.

"Go T go! Go T go!" the boys chanted.

"The important thing is this weekend," Paulo said. "We need to win the championship and make this the most perfect season of all time."

"We're Lions forever, and so are all the guys," Cody said. He felt a rush of emotion. "I've spent too much time thinking about the future. And it's dumb, because of anyone here I should know that doesn't help. What's important is what's happening now. Next season will come soon enough."

Kenneth held out his hand. Luca put his on top, then Paulo. Cody reached his hand out.

"First we win our quarter-final game," Kenneth said.

"Then we kick some Storm butt," Luca said.

"Especially Timothy's," Cody said.

"Lions on three!" Paulo said.

"One – two – three!"

"Roar!"

27

The Lions took the field. Cody steeled his nerve and forced himself to look calm. This game had to happen. Two teams on a collision course, as it should be. The Lions against the Storm — and the winner moved on to the finals. He quickly scanned the sidelines. John and Mitch stood together, but apart from the other Storm parents and players — and far away from Ian. Antonio's dad stood by himself.

"Storm Crush!" the Storm players chanted as they took their positions.

Trevor put a hand on Cody's shoulder. "You ready?"

"We've got this, Coach."

Trevor grunted, his eyes set firmly in a steely gaze. "We're going to need you for this one. Big game — and you can win it for us."

Cody wasn't sure how to react. "All the guys are psyched."

Trevor shook his head. "I've been thinking about your move to midfield. Stafa's got a striker's mentality. He's selfish, cocky, almost arrogant. He's ball-hungry. He thinks he's the best player out there and that he should take every shot. Strikers have to be like that. The second they begin to doubt themselves, they're done." Trevor looked Cody in the eye. "Does that sound like you?"

Cody crossed his arms and raised his eyebrows. "I . . . um . . . guess not. Not really."

"The best players know themselves to the core. The best players are the most honest players. They know what they can and cannot do on the field."

Cody let out a laugh.

Trevor smiled. "Why is that funny?"

"Sorry, Coach. It's not you. A few people have sorta asked me the same thing lately: Who are you, Cody?"

"Leandro's been on me to move you to midfield since he first saw you play," Trevor said, "I've wanted to do it too. But we didn't have anyone to take over the striker position. It was a no-brainer when Stafa came. You have striker speed and a knack for putting the ball in the net. But you're also thoughtful, sensitive, strong-willed, and courageous. You see the whole game. You pass well and have great foot skills. You belong in the middle of the action. And I believe you'll score your share of goals as well."

Cody wasn't used to Trevor's praise. Usually, Trevor was telling him what he was doing wrong.

"You can dominate this game," Trevor said. "You have

it in you. Don't rely on Paulo or Kenneth or Stafa. This is your game. The only thing holding you back is confidence."

"Thanks, Coach. I'll . . . try."

Trevor ran a hand across his chin. "It's been an honour to coach you, Cody. I know there's been a lot of . . . discussion about next season."

Cody waited for Trevor to say he should focus on this game and worry about that later. So what Trevor said next surprised him.

"It's hard for kids to appreciate that they're only young once," Trevor continued. "Trust me, the window on playing this game at the highest levels is small. And it's open to an equally small number of players. You're one of those players. Think long and hard before you sacrifice your talent. I'm the first one to admit that sports for kids has become too organized and intense. But sometimes a kid thrives under the competition and training. You could be that kid, if you want it."

The referee's whistle blasted to signal the start of the game. Cody's body warmed with a rising heat that went from his toes to the top of his head.

"By the way, what happened to your eye?" Trevor said.

"I hit myself . . . going around a corner in my house, a door."

Trevor grunted. Cody had the feeling Trevor didn't believe him.

"C'mon lads," Trevor yelled loudly, giving Cody a thump on the back. "Hard on every ball." He backed up to the sidelines.

"Ball possession," Leandro added. "Look for chances to attack."

The parents from both teams were chanting and clapping.

"Go Lions go!"

"Let's go Storm! Let's go!"

Cody took his spot to Kenneth's right. The Lions had the kickoff. Timothy drifted to his left.

"Yo, Humpty. I see you finally got off the ground," Timothy taunted.

"Maybe you should focus on your shoelaces," Cody said. He pointed at Timothy's cleats. "You wouldn't want to trip."

Timothy looked down. Kenneth, Jordan, and Paulo burst out laughing. Cody joined in. Of course, Timothy's laces were perfectly tied.

"Yeah, yeah, funny guy. Not as funny as punching you out," Timothy said.

"Maybe not," Cody said. "You did fall for the oldest trick in the book. Sorry to say, that makes you a total loser."

Stafa was listening closely. "You're that kid from the practice. I remember you. You really suck."

Timothy's eyes were blazing. His teammates all looked the other way.

"We'll see next year, punk. I've got five Premier teams ready to sign me," Timothy said to Stafa.

"Your dad is sponsoring five teams next year?" Kenneth said. "It would be cheaper for you to just stop playing."

The whistle sounded again and the referee held his arm over his head.

Cody took a moment. *Who was Cody Dorsett?* Tough

question. One thing he knew. He wasn't anyone's punching bag, and most definitely not Timothy's.

He also knew something else. He was going to do everything he could to win this game.

Stafa slipped the ball to Jordan to start the game. Jordan passed back to Kenneth, who gave it square to Cody. Cody faked a pass back to Luca. With Trevor's words in mind, he charged straight up the field, catching the Storm forwards on their heels. Timothy could only turn and give chase. Stafa presented himself twelve yards in front of the box.

"Use me," Stafa pleaded.

Typical striker, thought Cody. Stafa wanted the ball. But there were four defenders behind him — not the right time. So Cody feathered a diagonal pass to Paulo to the left. Paulo punched it back inside to Kenneth, who simply dummied the ball to Jordan, and he chipped it back to Paulo. Cody cut right and Paulo rewarded him with the perfect pass. Stafa head-faked right and broke left into the box. Now was the right time. Cody floated a right-footed cross in his direction. Stafa leapt and headed the ball to the Storm goalie's left, and only the goalie's desperate diving effort kept the ball out. The referee pointed to the corner flag. Jordan ran over to take it.

"Awesome cross, Cody," Stafa said, clapping in his direction.

The Lions poured into the box for the corner. Antonio marked Cody.

"I'll take that stiff," Timothy said.

"I got him," Antonio said.

Timothy stepped in between Antonio and Cody.

"Cover the post," the goalie told Antonio. "We don't need two guys covering the same guy."

Antonio glowered at Timothy and marched to the post. Timothy grinned and gave Cody a shove with his elbow.

"Need to call your mommy?" Timothy said.

Cody could see Timothy was more into chirping than defending. He ever so slightly turned his head toward Paulo and nodded to the area behind him. Paulo kicked his right heel. Jordan plucked some grass and threw it in the air like he was testing the wind — the return signal.

Jordan approached the ball. Cody leaned back and elbowed Timothy in the gut, then stomped on his right foot.

"Get lost, Egg-Head!" Timothy thundered.

He charged Cody and crashed his forearm into Cody's back. They both stumbled forward — leaving an open space behind them. Cody saw Paulo sneak into it. The ball flew overhead.

The crowd roared.

"Wake up, Storm," Ian raged from the sidelines. He slapped his clipboard on his thigh.

"What are you doing?" Antonio said to Timothy. "You were right there."

"Not my guy," Timothy shot back. "Tyler, he's yours."

Tyler grimaced and gave Timothy a vicious look.

"I knew he'd come after you," Paolo whispered to Cody gleefully.

They jogged back to their end. Timothy's boneheaded play had given the Lions an early lead. Unmarked right in front, Paulo had headed the ball into the net.

"Worth a slightly broken back," Cody said. "That was a sweet corner," he said to Jordan.

"Good call. I saw Timmer messing with you," Jordan said.

Brandon put an arm across Jordan's back. "One more corner like that and I might let you hang out with me again," Brandon said. Brandon and Jordan's falling-out earlier in the season had become a running joke between them.

"I'm going to keep making runs up the left side," Stafa said to Cody. "You and me, bro. We'll kill them."

Cody gave him a thumbs-up.

The referee put the ball on the dot. Timothy stepped forward.

"Let's play some soccer, Storm!" Timothy screamed.

He kicked the ball to the right, to the Storm's number nine. Too hard. It bounced over his foot. Stafa was on it like a shot. He and a midfielder collided just outside the circle and they both fell to the ground. Again, Cody was impressed. Stafa might be younger but didn't avoid the contact. He'd come to play. Cody didn't waste time cheering. He was closest to the ball. He took it on the run, with Paulo and Jordan flanking wide left. Two Storm midfielders were hustling to get back.

This time, ball possession seemed the smart play. They didn't have the manpower for a quick strike. He slowed and crossed the ball to Jordan on the left wing. Jordan gave it to Brandon, who gave it square to Kenneth inside, about ten yards from centre. Slowly, the Lions worked the ball up the left side, and then swung it to the right side. The Storm scurried across in defence, but to Cody they looked like they were just going through the motions. Antonio was playing hard, as he always did. The others looked like they didn't really care.

Paulo had the ball twenty feet from the box in the middle of the field. Kenneth went wide left. Brandon made a run up the left flank, and Ryan, the Lions left defender, came up to support. Stafa came across the top of the defence from right to left. Without warning, Paulo pushed forward, as if intent on crashing into a middle defender. Cody followed him, ten feet to his right. As always, Cody and Paulo knew exactly what the other wanted. But this time Stafa seemed to be able to read their minds, too. Five feet from pressure, with the Storm defence line determined to hold firm, Paulo left-footed a pass to Cody. Stafa dug his right foot into the ground, pivoted to face the Storm goal, and then pushed forward. Cody angled a soft one-timer between the two middle defenders. Stafa was onside, and in alone on goal.

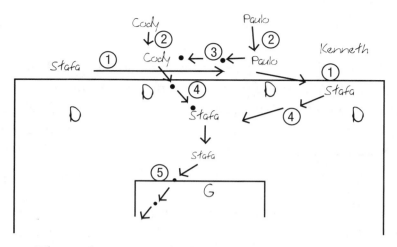

The goalie was caught deep in his net. Cody knew how Stafa felt: the ball under control, tons of net, the goalie at his mercy. It was a sweet feeling. But this time Cody felt better about being the guy who made the crucial pass. He was beginning to love being more involved in the play as a midfielder. He could use all his skills, and not just carry the ball a few feet and then shoot.

Stafa drove the ball to the right side. It went in about a foot inside the post. Cody jumped and threw his fist in the air. Stafa curled off toward the corner flag.

"Awesome strike," Cody yelled to Stafa.

They were a good team, he and Stafa, like he and Paulo. Timothy kicked at the ground, a few feet to Cody's right.

"You guys gonna play any defence today?" Timothy barked at his teammates.

Now was the time to test Timothy's breaking point, Cody figured.

"Nice kickoff, number ten," Cody said to Timothy. "I've never seen that. Are you sucking on purpose?"

Timothy's eyes narrowed.

"Sorry to hear you didn't get picked for the Premier

team. Benji said there's a rule about having losers on the team, so he had to cut you." Cody flicked his eyebrows and smiled.

"Not in my lifetime," Timothy hissed.

Timothy threw a punch at Cody's head. Cody was ready this time. He ducked and backed away. The Lions couldn't afford for him to be kicked out for fighting. He knew that. But he wasn't letting Timothy get in another cheap shot. One black eye was enough.

The referee's whistle blared. The ref ran over, fumbling in his shirt pocket.

"Did you see the elbow to my stomach on the corner?" Timothy yelled at the referee. "Open your freakin' eyes."

The referee pulled out a red card and held it over his head.

"You're gone, number ten," the referee said to Timothy.

"The guy pounds me in the stomach and *I'm* gone? You're such a tool," Timothy said.

"I'll catch up with you after the game, Timmer," Cody said.

"That's enough, or you can join him," the referee said to Cody.

Cody held his hands up. "I'm good."

He couldn't resist a grin. Earlier in the season Timothy had goaded him into taking a red card. It had cost the Lions that game. Even worse, the Lions had to forfeit the next game because with Cody's suspension, the Lions couldn't start eleven players. That had been a bitter lesson for Cody, but one well worth learning. In the biggest game of the season, Timothy would have to learn the same lesson.

"Sick pass," Stafa said to him, laughing, as Cody held a hand down low.

"Our friend Timothy has decided to sit the rest of the game out," Cody told his teammates. "They play with ten the rest of the way."

"What happened?" Kenneth said.

"He tried to give me matching black eyes," Cody said. "The ref didn't like it."

Ian had come onto the field. He pointed at Cody. "That midfielder mugged Timothy on the corner kick. How could you miss something so obvious? Then, when he defends himself against the same kid, you give Timothy, our best player, a red card? That's the dumbest call I've ever seen — ever. You have the IQ of a doorknob."

The referee pointed to the sidelines. "Off the field right now or I'll give you guys another red card and you can play two men down."

Ian was beet red. "I'll be talking to José about you," he said.

He whirled and went back to the sidelines.

Cody got into position for the kickoff. He'd never been more ready to play or more focused. The Lions were going to win this. He looked over to Ian. He was talking to some of the Storm parents. Cody wondered again about this José Ian kept mentioning.

The referee put the ball down for the kickoff.

"Ten guys. We control the ball, Lions," Cody called out. "Another goal and we're in the finals. Who wants it?"

The roar made it clear they all did.

29

Stafa had the ball at midfield. He faked left and whirled to the right side. Cody parked himself a few feet inside the Storm box. Stafa squared the ball to him. Cody took a few steps away from the net and chipped an easy pass right to where Kenneth was cutting to the sidelines.

Tweet!

Kenneth lofted the ball high into the box and jumped in the air.

7 – 0.

The Lions had not only beaten the Storm. They'd destroyed them. The team formed a huddle, slapping hands and pounding backs. It felt so good Cody couldn't contain his joy. He joined the pack, and as if on cue they began hopping up and down in rhythm.

"In the finals, boys," Kenneth said.

"One more," Luca said.

"No one can stop us now," Stafa said.

Finally, it broke up. Together, the happy boys made their way to their equally happy coaches, and behind them, a delirious bunch of parents.

"Lads, that was truly an inspirational effort," Trevor enthused. "The best game you've played all season."

"It was a pleasure to watch," Leandro said. "You should be proud of yourselves."

"We'll be proud when we win the championship," Stafa said.

"Lions on three!" Kenneth cried.

"One – two – three!"

"Roar!"

"That was an unexpected gift," Trevor said. "I didn't think they'd roll over like that."

An unwelcome voice interrupted.

"There's the Lions coach," Ian said, pointing out Trevor to another man. He was a bit taller than Ian, balding, and wore a black track suit with a yellow stripe down the sides.

"Can I help you?" Trevor said.

The man cleared his throat. He looked like he wanted to be somewhere else. "We've talked on the phone. I'm José Encarnacion, commissioner of the league." He cleared his throat again. "Ian has questioned the eligibility of one of your players."

The parents moved closer to listen in. Cody's ears perked up. So that's who José was. It figured Ian was buds with the league commissioner.

"I can assure you all our players are eligible," Trevor said.

"In fact, Ian used to be the Lions manager. He was in charge of that."

"Not for all the players," Ian said.

His smug smile gave Cody the creeps. To make it worse, Timothy was grinning from ear-to-ear. He looked like he was in on some private joke.

"I was asked about a certain player," José said. "First name is Paulo."

"That's my son," Leandro said.

"Can you confirm that Paulo played today?" José said.

"He's played a number of games, including today," Trevor said.

José's face fell. Cody's chest began to ache. There was something really bad going on. Ian's smile was getting way too big, and Timothy was outright laughing.

"Unfortunately, we've learned that Paulo never signed a waiver. The insurance company says that every player must sign. A player without a waiver is ineligible to play," José said.

Trevor's mouth opened momentarily. "But I included his name on every game sheet. You knew he was playing for us."

"Unfortunately, we didn't check. But the rules are clear." José snuck a glance at Ian.

"Serious trouble," Luca whispered to Cody.

"Ian registered Paulo," Trevor said. "I remember asking him, specifically, if the paperwork was done. He assured me it was."

"That's science fiction," Ian said. "I never said that, and I never took care of Paulo's waiver. He came for a tryout, and that's all I know. I quit as manager soon after. Your team isn't my responsibility, Trevor." He looked at José. "You overruled me and let Stafa play in this league. This time you have to disqualify them."

"Leandro, do you recall signing the waiver as Paulo's parent?" Trevor said.

"Certainly," Leandro said. "We met after practice and I signed all the papers. I absolutely signed a waiver because a player always has to sign one. We do the same thing back home."

"So go back home," Timothy said.

Ian laughed.

Trevor's face turned dark.

"There's nothing I can do," José said. He sounded upset. "The rule is clear. All players must sign a waiver, and we don't have a waiver for Paulo in the office. I just confirmed that."

"Then we'll sign one now," Leandro said.

"That would be fine for future games. But all games in which Paulo played before now will be forfeited," José said.

"Including today," Ian said triumphantly.

"You're out, Humpty, and we're in the finals," Timothy taunted Cody.

Benji pushed forward. "Now I get your game, Ian. I couldn't understand your threat before. You're the type of parent who ruins sports for kids."

"Yeah, whatever," Ian said. "I got no time for you."

"But you sure did when you wanted Timothy to play Premier. Then it was all sponsorship money and training in

Europe." Benji turned to Trevor. "I didn't understand him at the time, but he hinted that he could hurt the Lions any time he wanted, but he wouldn't if Timothy was striker for the Premier team. I didn't take him seriously. Besides, I'm not that type of coach. I choose the best players, not the players parents pay me to choose."

The Lions parents had gathered around, with Trevor and Leandro in front. They began talking all at once.

"Totally unfair."

"He's responsible."

"Ian did it on purpose."

José held his hands up. "I really feel bad. I do. All games Paulo played must be forfeited. The Storm will advance to the finals against United. That's it."

Ian and Timothy high-fived.

"Boo hoo. Too bad, so sad," Timothy said to the Lions.

"You can't play, Timothy. You got a red card," Kenneth said. "You're suspended for at least one game."

"Not true," Ian said. "The game was forfeited, which means it never happened. The red card has been overturned."

Timothy winked at Cody. "Of course, you ran away like a chicken from me today. Like you did yesterday."

"Try it now," Cody said. He felt a rage growing inside him. Ian had set them up.

"Later, little boys," Timothy said. "I gotta get ready for the finals tomorrow."

The coaches, parents, and José began arguing. Timothy and Ian left.

"Guys, this is . . ." Paulo couldn't finish.

"Not your fault," Cody said. He struggled to hold back

his tears. He felt sick to his stomach.

"The season's over? Just like that?" Luca said. "Ian and Timothy win?"

"It's like Voldemort beats Harry Potter in the last movie," Kenneth said. "No one wants to see that."

"It's like a waste of a season," Stafa said.

Cody couldn't accept that. He could accept that Ian was a snake and tricked Trevor into believing Paulo was registered properly. Cody bet Ian had been waiting all season to do this. He could also accept Timothy's cheap shot. That was Timothy being Timothy. He couldn't — he wouldn't — accept the idea that this season was for nothing.

"We won the game. We won," Cody said. "And we did it the right way, like a team. We did what no one said we could do. Play with eleven guys. Have Stafa come from a younger league and join the team. Make the playoffs. We made the finals, and everyone on the Storm knows it. If they want to lose to United because of Ian's garbage, then let them. Doesn't mean anything to me. And it doesn't matter where any of us play next year either. You'll always be my teammates."

Cody held out his hand. Kenneth and Luca added theirs. It didn't take long for everyone to put a hand in.

"We all need to call it," Cody said.

"Lions on three!" they shouted.

30

Cody looked on glumly. He'd come to watch Mandy and Talia's final game, which they won 3 − 1. Then, as if some magnetic force wouldn't let him leave, he'd stayed to watch the final between United and the Storm. Kenneth and Luca were there too.

Timothy knocked the ball to his inside right midfielder for the kickoff. Two United forwards ran up to pressure. The Storm midfielder sent it across to the centre midfielder, who one-timed it to Antonio on the back line. Antonio drifted left with the ball and then punched a line drive up the left sideline to a waiting forward.

"I think Paulo's off to the airport soon, in an hour or two," Kenneth said.

"You think we'll ever see him again. I mean, really?" Luca said.

"Not sure," Kenneth said. "Not like I can just say 'Hey, Mom, I'm going to bike over to Paulo's house. Be back in two months.'"

"This is so bogus," Cody said. "Paulo leaves and we have to forfeit. Life owes us — big time."

"I knew it would suck to watch this game," Kenneth said. "I didn't know it would be so unbelievably painful that I would have to fly into a mad rage and scream and yell — and need to beat Luca around the head and shoulders."

"Don't bottle your feelings up," Luca said. "If you need to beat me, go for it."

"Actually, Cody might be fun to attack, too" Kenneth said. He stomped his foot on the ground. "Now I don't know what to do."

"Ask the girls," Luca said, nodding to his right.

Mandy and Talia each wore their team track suit and had a backpack slung over her shoulder. Their gold medals bounced off their chests with each step. Mandy's braids weren't tied up in her usual ponytail, and some of them had coloured beads. Cody thought it made her look different — a bit fancier.

"Talia, should I pummel Luca or Cody?" Kenneth said.

"I think they should pummel you," Talia said.

"Listen to Miss I'm-So-Amazing-'Cause-My-Team-Won-the-Championship-this-Morning," Kenneth said.

Cody sidled up to Mandy. "Awesome game," he said.

"Thanks. The girls all came through."

"You sort of came through with those two goals," he said.

She laughed. "It's a team game," she said.

Mandy looked around and then stepped a few yards

to the side. She motioned for Cody to follow where the others couldn't hear.

"Mom told me you spoke to her yesterday," she said simply.

"Yeah. Saw her before your first game."

"It was nice of you to talk to her."

"Why wouldn't I talk to her?"

She gathered her braids in her hand and then let them fall. "No reason . . . Just . . . thanks. It meant a lot to her . . . and to me."

"How's she doing? Is she getting ready to leave the hospital?"

"I think so. At least, soon. The doctors don't want to rush things, and I guess that makes sense. But it would be nice if she could . . . nice if things could be normal. Or at least a bit more normal."

"Well done, Marco!" they heard Kenneth yell.

The United defender had drilled a left-footed strike into the top corner for the first goal of the game. They all cheered United, as the players drifted back into position.

"Don't just stand around and watch!" Timothy screamed at the Storm defence. "The point is to try to stop him."

Antonio stood in front of the box, hands on his hips. He glared at Timothy. Tyler and Michael kept their heads down and said nothing.

"Let's get it back, Timmer," Ian called from the sidelines.

"Get it back yourself!" Timothy raged.

"Timothy's being a jerk. Some things are normal," Cody observed.

"Not exactly what I meant. But maybe it's a start," Mandy said.

She gathered her braids in her hand again. Her mom's bracelets sparkled in the sun. Cody reached for her gold medal and rubbed the surface with his fingers.

"Nice hardware . . . Although you're showing off by wearing it in front of me," he said.

"I want you to be impressed," she said.

"I am impressed," he said.

That came out a little too seriously, thought Cody. He turned to watch the game. He had a feeling his face had turned red.

"What are you up to this afternoon?" he said, to change the subject.

She tilted her head and pursed her lips. "There's talk of having a sleepover tonight at Talia's, with the girls on the team."

"Sounds good."

"Yeah. It will be. It's always awkward at the end of a season. Some girls are leaving the team. A few always do. Without soccer, sometimes it turns out we don't have that much in common." Mandy lowered her chin, and with a glance at Cody, slowly shook her head a few times. "Typical Mandy, being negative. The girls are cool, and everything will be fine. Don't know why I need to do that."

Cody had secretly hoped that Mandy would hang a bit with him — and Kenneth, Luca, and Talia.

"What are you guys doing?" she said.

He shrugged. "Probably not much. Paulo's gone, or he's leaving today, anyway. A couple of other guys have left on holidays. Kenneth and David are leaving for the Premier team. The Lions have broken up already."

"The forfeit still bugs me," Mandy said. "That Ian guy is unbelievable."

"Some people always get their way," Cody said. "Ian never has to answer for what he does. Timothy either."

"That reminds me of someone — someone who doesn't pay what he owes," she said.

"Who?"

"Well . . . kinda . . . Cody Dorsett."

He stared at her in shock.

"The ice cream? Like, how convenient that you forgot."

He squeezed his lips together and gave her a cold look. "I was planning on inviting you tomorrow. But you might be too rude a girl."

"You have no idea," she said dryly. "But I accept the invitation anyway."

"Did I actually invite you?" he said.

"You did."

"What time did we plan to meet?"

She put her finger to her lips. "I think we said three o'clock."

"I'm picking the flavours, though. We can't have another banana-split disaster," he said.

"Please! I ordered like a mad genius."

"I'll give you the mad part."

"Shush," she said, her eyes back on the field.

Timothy cut across the top of the box with the ball. He planted his right foot for a kick. Marco leapt just as he shot. The ball nicked Marco's thigh and bounced to a United defender, and he calmly knocked the ball out of harm's way.

Mandy tugged on his sleeve. "Cody, what are we?" she said.

"Like . . . What do you mean?" he said.

He had a feeling he knew, but he was too nervous to say it.

"You and me. Are we friends? Are we more than friends? Talia keeps telling me that we are and . . . I'm not sure. I get that we haven't known each other long — and this thing with Mom would freak any boy out. And it's cool, whatever you think. Only . . . it's bugging me and . . . Well, that's the question."

Cody felt like a thousand spotlights were blazing down on him. "I guess . . . we're friends, for sure."

She nodded and lowered her eyes.

"But . . . I wouldn't mind if we were . . . like . . . good friends. Or special friends, if that's what you meant," he said.

She looked up at him and crinkled her nose. "Yeah, that's sorta what I meant."

He knew his face was all red, but he didn't look away this time.

"It's nice to talk to someone who understands you," she said. "You've been awesome since we met. The Marathon Game and telling me about your cancer and listening to me about Gavin and Mom . . . I can't tell you how important it was to me." Her eyes twinkled. "All you need to do is learn something about ice cream and we'll be good."

"Are we about to have our first fight?" he said.

"No, I'll let you pick the flavours tomorrow. I owe you that. But it'll be the last time."

"I better put some thought into it. I don't want to waste my only chance to eat quality ice cream."

She didn't laugh. She looked happy though, and that made him happy.

He was surprised to realize he was happy. Sure, it was hard to watch the Storm playing in the final. But that wasn't a reason to be sad. One thing he'd learned this summer was how much he loved the game of soccer, but that even soccer wasn't the most important thing in the world compared to family and friends.

"Go United go! Go United go!" Kenneth and Luca began chanting.

Cody joined in, and so did Talia and Mandy.

It was late in the first half. United had pumped five goals in already. The Storm had basically given up. Timothy and Ian hadn't stopped screaming and yelling, but no one else seemed all that interested.

"Don't you guys ever get tired of soccer?"

That was Paulo's voice!

Cody turned around. Paulo held his arms out and grinned. "I made my dad swing by the field. I knew you'd be here. Had to say goodbye one last time. We're off to the airport."

"Do you know this guy?" Kenneth said to Luca.

"He seems familiar, but I can't recognize the face," Luca said.

"I'm that awesome, cool guy who played on the Lions," Paulo said.

"That's impossible. I'm the awesome, cool guy on the Lions," Kenneth said.

"Hold on, does awesome and cool mean the same thing as being a big doofus?" Luca said.

Kenneth peered up to the sky. "Not sure — I think so."

"You boys are so lame," Talia said. She went over and gave Paulo a hug. "You have to promise, and I mean it, to come back soon and visit."

"I will," Paulo said.

Mandy gave him a hug as well. "We're going to miss you," she said.

"Take care of these boys for me," Paulo said. "They're pathetic, I know. But they've learned to tie their own shoelaces, so there's hope."

"You can tie your own laces?" Kenneth said to Luca.

"My mom does them," Luca said. "Don't tell him."

"Your mom can do laces?" Kenneth said.

There was a pause. Instead of being full of laughter, Paulo's eyes were heavy and red. He blinked a few times. "*Até mais*," he said. "That means 'See you later' in Portuguese."

"*Até mais*," they answered.

Cody stepped forward. "Take care of yourself, Paulo. It was great hanging out this summer."

Paulo hesitated. Then he gave Cody a hug — and after that Luca and Kenneth did too.

A car horn sounded.

Paulo pointed to the field and flicked his eyebrows. "We would've totally crushed United," he said.

He began to walk to the parking lot, but about twenty

yards away he stopped. He flashed two finger guns at them all, and offered his classic toothy grin.

Cody flashed two finger guns back. They all did.

Then Paulo got in the car and was gone.

Cody had to give his head a shake. How could Paulo be gone?

Kenneth elbowed Luca in the ribs.

"We need to save this situation," Kenneth said. "Too much sadness. I don't want to start crying in front of the G - I - R - L - S."

"What does that spell?" Luca asked Cody.

Cody shook his head. "I'm just a kid. How would I know?"

"How about a sleepover? One where we agree to go to sleep but really stay up all night and then make our parents' lives miserable the next day," Kenneth said. "I'll call my folks and set it up."

"Could we combine that with Movie Madness and excessive junk food?" Luca said.

"That's included in the definition of *sleepover*," Kenneth said.

"Go United!" Talia yelled suddenly.

United had scored again off a corner kick. The score was 6 – 0. United barely celebrated. Instead, most of them were laughing and joking around, like they couldn't take the competition seriously.

Timothy kicked at the ground, his face beet red.

"Just get one back, Timmer," Ian said. "Not your fault. You can't win yourself. No one else came out to play. You're doing awesome."

The whistle blew to end the first half.

"It's fun to watch the Storm getting hammered. But at the same time it's incredibly dull and boring. You guys wanna head back to my place? We can get started on the movie marathon," Kenneth said.

"The girls are coming to my house later," Talia said, "But I wouldn't mind a warm-up."

"I've seen enough hammering," Luca said. "Sounds like a plan."

The United players jogged off the field to loud cheers from their parents and friends. The Storm supporters watched in stony silence.

Instead of heading off with his team, Marco ran to Cody and his friends.

"Hey, guys, I'm glad you're here. I wanted to talk to you for a sec," Marco said.

"I'm loving the score," Kenneth said to Marco. "Could you get about fifteen more? It's been a dream of mine to see the Storm humiliated in the finals after they cheated to get in."

"Glad to do you the favour." Marco laughed. "Feels good to pump in a bunch in the first half. Maybe it will shut that Timothy up. Anyway, we heard about the league defaulting you guys. Totally unfair. Everyone knows Ian did it on purpose. I mean, he was your manager when that Paulo kid joined your team." He paused and shook his head in disgust. "Anyway, the boys want to know if you can get the Lions together for the real, unofficial championship game. We should be playing you guys, not the Storm."

"Sounds great," Kenneth said. "But we don't have a full team. Paulo just left to go back to Brazil. And two other guys are gone tomorrow on holiday."

"We're in," Cody said, an idea forming in his mind. "We'll find eleven players."

"Awesome," Marco said. "Do you guys know the park with the tennis courts?"

"You mean the one with the basketball court at the one end?" Cody said.

That was where he'd met Paulo.

"Yup. Let's meet there tomorrow at twelve o'clock," Marco said. "We'll play the regulation ninety minutes and call our own fouls. Total bragging rights are on the line."

"Twelve it is," Kenneth said.

Marco and Kenneth slapped hands, and Marco went back to join his teammates.

"Don't forget. Fifteen more," Kenneth said to him.

Marco held a thumbs-up over his head.

"We're three guys down," Kenneth said to Cody. "What's the plan?"

"First, we're *two* players down, because we have Austin, so that gives us nine," Cody said. "Second, all we have to do is find *two more* players. Maybe a striker and a midfielder?"

Kenneth and Luca started laughing.

"So where could we possibly find two great players on short notice?" Cody said.

He began to look around.

"When did Cody start thinking he was hilarious?" Talia said.

"When did I stop?" Cody said.

"Then we have the starting eleven," Kenneth said. "C'mon everyone, follow me. To the Batmobile!"

They looked at him.

"I guess that would make more sense if we had a Batmobile. And if I had a driver's licence," Kenneth said. He put a finger in the air. "How about — to our bicycles!"

Kenneth began to run to where they'd locked their bikes, skipping and flapping his arms furiously like a bat. Luca and Talia were right behind, skipping and flapping along.

"Why do we put up with these idiots?" Mandy said.

"Because they're the only idiots we've got." Cody grinned.

He started skipping and flapping his arms — with Mandy right beside him.

Cody put his backpack down in the hallway.

"I'm going to get going," he said.

"You just got home and now you're running off?" his mom said.

"Kenneth is having a sleepover. Dad said it's okay."

His dad came into the living room. "What did I say?"

"That I could go to Kenneth's."

"Impossible. I'd never say anything so ridiculous." He laughed.

"Okay, Dad," Cody said, but he had to laugh. His father could be funny too. Ran in the family, maybe.

"Could you hold up for one minute?" his mom said. "We just want to talk to you — very quickly."

"Yeah. Sure."

Cody sat on the couch. His parents took the seats across

from him. He felt a rush of nerves. It looked like they wanted to talk about something serious.

"Who won the final?" his dad said.

They wanted to talk about the game?

"United," Cody said. "We left at half-time. It was already 6 – 0. It was fun to see. Paulo came and said goodbye, too."

"Nice you had a final chance to say goodbye," his mom said. "Anyway, Trevor called me and we had a nice chat this morning. He's decided to coach the Lions next season, and he was asking if you'd made a decision. He said some wonderful things about you. He said you were more than welcome to come back, but it was up to you, naturally. As for Benji, I'm really getting tired of screening my calls and not answering his texts. You can't keep stringing him along."

Cody flopped back. "I'm tortured. If we don't go to Ferguson, half of me wants to play Premier and the other half wants to stay with the Lions. I keep asking myself why I want to play Premier. Not like I'm going to get a scholarship or play pro."

"You don't know that," his mom said.

"C'mon, Mom. Let's be real. Look at Stafa. He's a year younger — and he's a way better striker than me."

"Everyone's different," Cheryl said. "He's developed physically faster than you. You have abilities that he doesn't. Maybe the difference between you is confidence."

"I don't know," Cody murmured. Of course his mom would think that. Parents always believe their own kids are amazing.

"Is soccer affecting your feelings about moving?" his dad said.

Cody weighed his words carefully. "Maybe I'm tired of change. We moved here because I got sick, and we went through all that. And then the drama with trying out and Timothy and Ian, a new coach, players quitting, and the Marathon Game. And of course, to top it off, Paulo leaving and Kenneth and David playing Premier." He squeezed his hands between his knees. "You can tell me that's just life and nothing ever stays the same. Somehow that doesn't help."

"We didn't want to burden you with this before Championship Weekend," his mom said, "But we really need to make some decisions. School starts in a week. We can't sell our house before then, but we could rent something in Ferguson and get you enrolled in your old school. If that's what you want."

"It might be fun to go back," Cody said.

"On the other hand, while it's always a bit unnerving to go to a new school, I'm sure you'd settle in here soon enough," his dad said.

"I agree, there's that," his mom said. "Ferguson is smaller, and there's the question of whether we want to be in a bigger place. A small town is nice to grow up in."

"Probably more to do here," his dad said, "especially for Cody."

"Ferguson's not the middle of nowhere," she said.

"I know. Just saying a bigger town has more facilities," he said.

"I don't do much — soccer and school," Cody said.

"You will." His dad chuckled. "Not sure I'm looking forward to the teenage years."

"Sean, what do you want?" his mom said.

His dad gripped the arms of his chair. "I'll be happy with whatever works best for Cody. Business-wise, it's probably better for me to be here. But I can make it work from Ferguson. It'll just mean a bit more driving time. What about you?"

His mom's eyes got glossy. "I miss my family in Ferguson. Not that I don't love being close to your sister Beth and her kids."

"Would we actually miss Adam and Sarah if we moved back to Ferguson?" Cody joked.

"Yes, we would miss them. They're your cousins," she said with a smile.

For a moment no one said anything. His parents both looked at him.

Soccer — school — friends — change. His mind whirled.

"How do you feel, Cody?" his mom said.

"We want you to be honest with us," his dad said.

"I guess . . . if I had to vote . . ."

Cody thought about Kenneth and Luca and everything that had happened here — and Mandy. "I think I might want to stay. Do we really need to make the final decision now? I could go to my new school here and try it out. If it's really bad, then maybe we could go to Ferguson. Would that work?"

"Sounds like a sensible plan," his dad said. "What do you think, Cheryl?"

She didn't answer right away. "I most of all needed to hear what Cody and you wanted. I didn't want you guys to just go along with me about Ferguson. Absolutely, let's see how this school year goes, then we'll decide."

"You won't miss your family too much?" Cody said to her. He worried he'd hurt her feelings.

"Cody, you and your dad *are* my family. I want what's best for you. If you want to give your new school a chance, then I'm one hundred per cent behind it. Besides, Ferguson is only a couple hours away."

"Which brings us to the next question. What about the soccer team?" his dad said.

Cody looked out the window.

"You have to decide," his mom said. "I'm going to text Benji and Trevor that you'll tell them by tomorrow night. If you still can't decide, I'll say you're staying with the Lions. It's unfair to Benji. He'll want to sign someone else if you turn down the offer."

Cody got up. "That sounds fair. I'll decide. I promise." He went to the hallway and picked up his backpack. "Thanks, guys . . . for everything. You take good care of me."

"Oh, Cody . . ."

His mom came over and gave him a hug. Then his dad joined them for a group hug.

"Think about what you want for yourself," his mom said. "It boils down to the type of person you want to be. Neither choice is wrong. Depends on where you want to put your energy."

That sounded like familiar advice.

"You'll be happy to know we're not going to Auntie Beth's tomorrow for dinner," his mom said.

"Hooray, no Adam and Sarah." Cody threw his fist into the air.

"They're coming here," she said.

He slowly lowered his fist. "Hooray," he squeaked.

"Cody?"

"I'm kidding, Mom. That's cool."

"Give me a call when you get to Kenneth's," she said.

"Mom! It's, like, a ten-minute bike ride."

"Cody, I need to know you got there."

"Dad?"

"It wouldn't hurt to call," his dad said softly.

It wouldn't, and it would make her feel better. "Okay, Mom. No problem."

"Thanks, Cody. Have fun."

He went to get his bike. Life seemed to be whizzing by. The soccer season was over. Paulo was gone. School was starting in a week. And he and Mandy were . . . What had they called it? Special friends?

Wait until Kenneth and Luca heard about that.

He got on his bike.

They'd find out tonight — because he was going to tell them.

The ball bounced off a United midfielder's shin. Cody leapt at it and was able to knock it to the right with his cleats. Both players spun at the same time, but Cody was a hair faster.

"Yo, Cody," Stafa called.

Cody stabbed the ball with his toe to get it to his teammate. Stafa dribbled to the left and send it wide right to Mandy. Stafa and Cody followed the pass, with Cody hanging back to give Mandy a safe outlet. The ever-present Marco came up to cover Stafa. Mandy hesitated only a moment before rolling a crisp pass to Cody. He quickly assessed the situation.

For a pickup game, the pace had been relentless, probably because there were no refs. Back and forth the play raged. So far, deep in the second half, there had been just one goal for United, an unlucky deflection off William that skidded between David's legs on a corner. It had been an incredibly tight, competitive game.

Cody was tired, and he figured United would be too. It was time to push it. He ragged the ball inside — and then surprised everyone by back-heeling it outside to Mandy. She roared down the right wing, leaving United's left mid-fielder behind. Stafa presented himself about twenty yards in front of their net. Talia had come over to support as well, a bit to Stafa's right. Ryan had camped out on the far side of field.

Mandy stepped over the ball and brought it outside with her right foot. Marco collapsed down low to cut her off from the net. United's goalie came out to take away the angle, and the other two defenders swung over. Stafa backed up to put himself squarely in front of the net, no more than ten yards from the goal line, readying himself for a cross. Ryan pushed forward also, and Kenneth raced over for a short pass.

All his life Cody had seen the game as a forward, at the top of the play looking back. It had been almost like there were two games going on. The first game was the mid-fielders and defenders fighting over the ball, racing about in a mad scramble. The second was the cat-and-mouse game he played with the back line to get open for a shot or a run on goal.

Playing midfielder had totally opened Cody's mind to the game. A midfielder had to be more like a chess player, always thinking strategy. He had to know what was going on all over the field. He also had to figure out what to do with the ball. Plus, he had to think about himself and where he needed to be on the field — not to mention defence.

Sometimes Cody used to daydream during those long stretches when the other team controlled the ball and he hung near centre waiting for a turnover. Midfield was all-absorbing. He could never lose focus.

He was beginning to love it, and to wonder why he had been so upset about moving back.

That fear of change thing?

He wasn't going to be that guy ever again.

He also wasn't going to be afraid of going to a new team. Suddenly, he knew that's what Cody Dorsett needed to do. This was about the most fun he'd ever had playing soccer. United was a tough, skilled squad.

Premier would be even harder. That would make it even more fun.

Tournaments, practices, games — bring it on. Cody needed to find out what he was made of. Maybe he didn't know himself exactly yet, but he was making progress!

Cody snuck past a United player into an empty spot thirty yards from the net. He no longer felt tired. This is what he loved to do: play soccer. And nothing was better than playing in the park without refs and adults and whistles and commissioners — and managers who cheat with registrations.

This was pure soccer.

Mandy stutter stepped and spun away from the net, the ball still under the control of her dancing feet. Marco stayed back. He and the other United players had learned the hard way to respect her skills. A few had been left looking foolish after charging right at her when she had the ball.

Mandy hesitated again and pulled the ball back with her left foot. Talia swept across the box with her hand over her head. Stafa ran toward Mandy, also calling for it. Both strikers wanted a chance to score. Mandy looked over to Cody. He knew what she wanted.

He dashed to his right to put himself closer to the goal. Mandy chipped the ball over a United player's head. The quick pass meant there was a gap on the short side between Marco and the outside right defender. A striker wouldn't have seen that standing up by the back line.

Cody volleyed the ball with his right leg, putting a bit of outside spin on it. The ball curled wide and then cut sharply to the net. The United goalie dove to his left, both hands stretched overhead. The ball dipped and bounced inside the orange pylon to the back of the net.

The Lions players let out a collective roar. Marco hung his head for a moment and then looked up, a big grin on his face.

"Do we need to start worrying about overtime rules?" Marco said.

"Let's play golden goal," Stafa said. "Sudden death."

Cody shook his head. "Let's do two fifteen-minute halves," he said. "This game is too fun to end. Besides, we'll use our fitness to crush United into dust."

Stafa held out his hand, and Cody slapped it.

"I forgot how out of shape these guys are. Good plan," Stafa said. He held his hand out to Mandy next. "You should play with us next season. Both of you." He nodded at Talia.

Talia gave Cody a high-five. "Nice shot. What took you so long to score?"

"I hate showing off," Cody said.

Marco laughed and he slapped hands with Cody.

"Looking forward to playing with you," Marco said.

He obviously didn't know Cody hadn't signed yet.

"I'm pretty psyched about it too," Cody said. "Benji seems like a nice coach, and I think it's a good group of guys."

"As long as that Timothy ain't playing, I'm good," Marco said.

"I'm with you on that," Cody said. They slapped hands again.

"Now get lost — and no more scoring," Marco said.

"Can't promise that. I've always dreamed of an overtime marker," Cody said.

Marco flicked his chin and jogged back to his goalie.

Mandy came over. "You can't live in Ferguson if you're playing on the Premier team," she said.

"Why would I live in Ferguson?" Cody said. "Sometimes you say really random stuff. Like when you order ice cream. You make no sense."

"I was going to let you order this afternoon. But now that you're being rude, you've lost the right," Mandy said.

"Does that mean more mocha almond fudge?" he moaned.

"Depends on if I let you have any," she said.

"I don't care," Cody said. "It'll be fun anyway."

"Don't get serious on me. I like the funny Cody," Mandy said.

Cody laughed. He liked the funny Cody too.

"Nice strike, young man," Luca yelled from the back line.

Cody waved back. "This is our time, Lions," he called out. "We keep pushing it. Our game. We just have to want it more. Lions on three! One – two – three!"

"Roar!" his teammates thundered back.

"United!" Marco said.

"Hu!"

"United!" he repeated.

"Hu!"

"We are United!" they chanted.

Stafa took his spot near centre. He clapped over his head a few times. "Stay sharp, boys. Hard on every ball."

Stafa and Talia slapped hands.

"Hey, United, if you guys let me score, I'll let you carry me off the field like a hero and then we can all talk about how amazing I am," Kenneth said.

The United forwards laughed. One of them put the ball down. He turned to face his teammates.

"Are we champions?" he said. "This is when we prove it."

Cody readied himself. He looked around. Mandy was crouched, bent slightly forward, hands by her sides. Stafa and Talia were leaning toward the United end, about to blast off with the kickoff. Kenneth was bouncing from one foot to another, staring at the ball. Luca had his hands on his thighs, looking straight ahead.

The Lions were ready.

United played it back to their inside right midfielder. Talia and Stafa charged in pursuit.

So there it was. He wasn't going to Ferguson. He would play Premier. Funny how simple it ended up being.

United played the ball to the right side. Cody broke for it and went in hard for a tackle. He knocked it away from the United midfielder's feet. Mandy trapped it and played it square to Kenneth. Cody got back up, just in time to take a pass from Kenneth. Stafa and Talia raced forward. Cody pushed the ball up field. He had Ryan in support on his left, with Luca making a run of his own inside. On the right, Mandy was working to get free for a pass.

He decided to keep the ball a little longer and see what developed. Cody Dorsett was going to make something happen.